ALBERT PARK

A MEMOIR IN LIES

Minneapolis

First Edition January 2025
Albert Park. Copyright © 2025 by Susan Bernadette Koefod.
All rights reserved.

This is a work of fiction. All of the characters, names, incidents, organizations, and dialogue are either the products of the author's imagination or are used fictitiously.

10 9 8 7 6 5 4 3 2 1
ISBN: 978-1-962834-33-9

Cover and book design by Gary Lindberg

ALBERT PARK

A MEMOIR IN LIES

SUSAN KOEFOD

CALUMET
EDITIONS
Minneapolis

Also by Susan Koefod

<u>The Arvo Thorson Series</u>

Washed Up

Broken Down

Burnt Out

<u>Young Adult</u>

Naming the Stars

For everyone who believed in me and my stories

Prologue

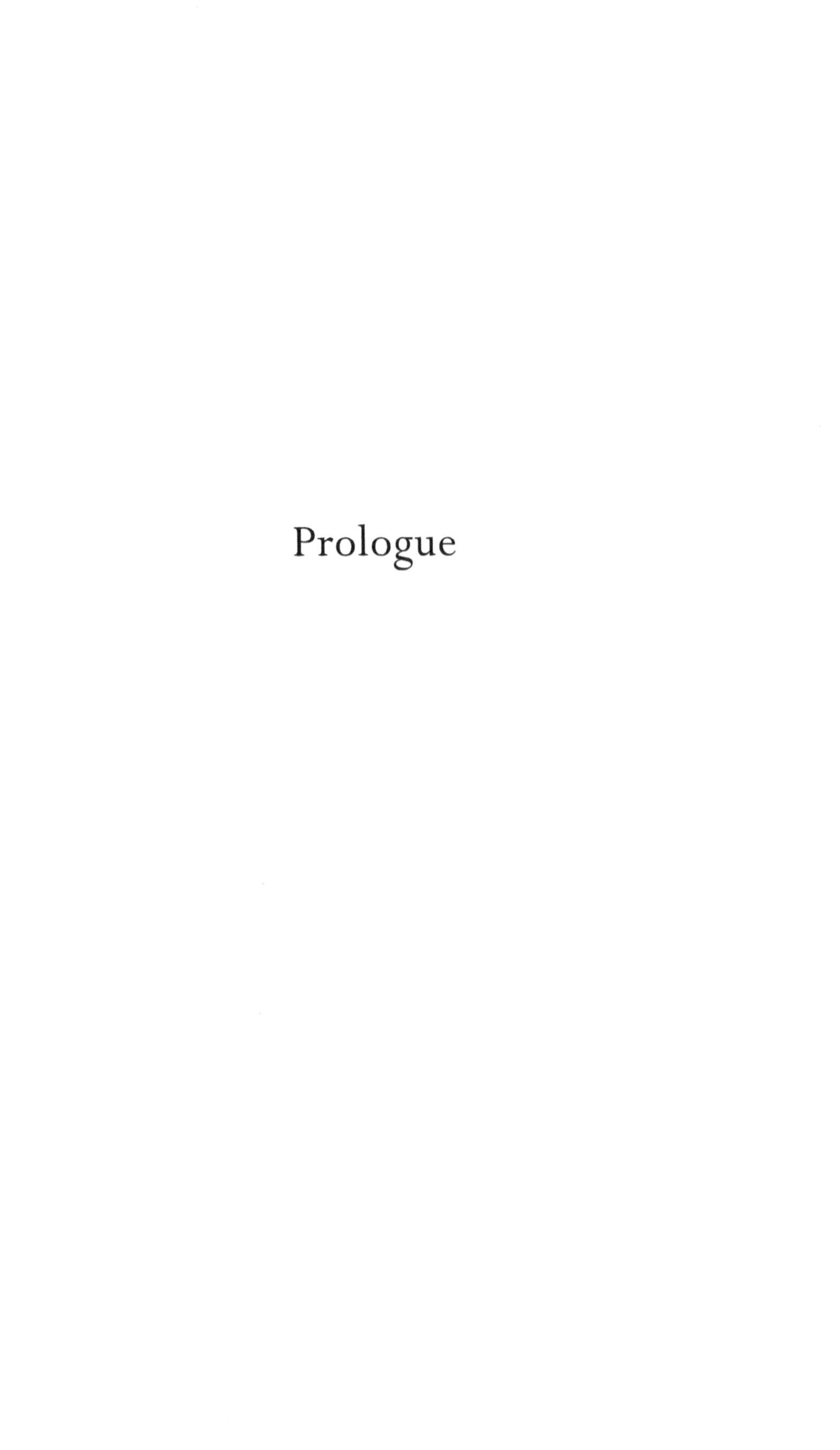

Remember

Everything about Albert Park is a lie. Beginning with his name.

This is the first thing anyone will tell you about me.

Regardless, I will start with a fact. Something that everyone can agree upon.

There is a place called Albert Park. It lies in a triangle of land bordered by a strip mall, a dry cleaner and a service garage. According to the plaque affixed to the monument there (a thirty-foot high obelisk modeled after the Washington Memorial), it is the world's smallest dedicated park. This designation is listed in *Ripley's Believe It or Not*. Look it up. Drive there and see it for yourself.

I was deposited in Albert Park as an infant, a quivering pink piece of flesh wrapped in a foreign language newspaper. It was in front of the plaque and below the flagpole where the people who took me in found me.

I was not sweetly swaddled in a soft reed basket like some Moses but packed in a cardboard box and dropped off by the post office. I still have the postmark from that box. There was no return address. I know that many wish there was, because I have often been told to go back where I came from.

Albert Park became my name because I had no name, no past, no one I belonged to.

Late in October of 1957, I was mailed there from San Francisco by someone unknown. In my research to determine my true origin, I learned that had I been mailed across the country a few months earlier—July, let's say. I would have sweltered and died on the way to Minnesota, arriving a bloated, fetid corpse in a stained onesie. Any later and I'd have arrived frozen and dead, perhaps less fetid, but a corpse no less.

So, I started out with the good fortune to have been mailed under temperate conditions. Perhaps it was the bad fortune of others that I lived, for all the grief everyone says I have caused—starting with the scientists who took me in.

The people who found me, and with whom I spent my early years, were not alerted to my existence by wailing infant cries or the stink of my unchanged diaper. They needed a sturdy box to mail their manuscript—a long and still unpublished study of their theory of the earth as a squishy blob in the grip of an anxious, overworked deity.

The day I came to Albert Park, as the scientists were struggling with their unbound manuscript and other research materials at a nearby bus stop, they noticed a good-sized, serviceable box not more than a few feet away.

That the box had arrived in such excellent condition—thanks to the still robust nature of its contents—made it appear perfect for their need.

After their discovery of me, they never mentioned to anyone what they thought of the contents. For all I know, they may have wept with joy to see me. They were childless and still very young. They had fallen even deeper in love during those long hours when they worked side by side developing complex calculations on matching slide rules. They may have been trying to have a baby, without much success.

I only know that I lived with them for the first five years of my life, and even in those years, I caused them no end of heartache. I was no comfort to them, people later told me, and they needed comfort. I cried, screamed and kicked. As soon as I could talk, I told hurtful lies. I broke their slide rules and ruined their carefully prepared models by stabbing the small balloons they filled with sand to demonstrate their theories.

My bad behavior aside, the manuscript and their life work were never taken seriously. Cartoonists pictured them as a pair of clown punching bags with enormous bulging eyes. They were ridiculed so mercilessly that they had to flee the country. They left me, probably with much relief, in a foundling's home before jetting off to their asylum. A small plane carrying them to the Peruvian mountain village they planned to call home crashed in a 100-year storm and their bodies were never recovered.

I want to set my story straight, tell it as I know it—or rather, as I judge the truth of it. I can rely only on my memory, for no one survives who will speak to me of my early history, and others are too frightened to talk of the terrible things they say I have done to them.

Some people will say it is impossible for Albert Park to tell the truth about anything. While this may be true, everyone knows that even the most faithful memory can never be a complete replica of an original life event—no more than the single raindrop can be recovered intact from its puddle. It's pointless to argue about the truth of memories.

Many have already made up their minds about me and will choose not to listen to anything else that I have to say. So be it. I will tell my story in my way, not to defend myself or to prove anything.

I will tell my story because I lie awake at night with the fragments of it piercing me as if my bed was littered with broken glass.

I will tell my story because I must remove each shard and hold each to the light.

I will tell my story because I must piece together each jagged bit and see for myself the shattered image I have become.

Part 1: Lies of Omission

Chapter 1—Entombed

What I remember most about the foundling home were the "coffins:" our sturdy, high-walled beds where we were locked away each night like unwanted toys. There was no escape once you were inside. No way out should a predator come prowling. A death trap. That's what made them coffins.

I hardly remember anymore what the outside of the home looked like since we were rarely taken out. Then, when it burned down, I never saw the orphanage again. Mr. Peter and I went away. But I'm getting ahead of myself.

The coffin room was large, probably the largest room in that drafty old house. Mr. Peter—a defrocked priest—and his wife, Mrs. Mary—a former nun—ran the foundling home. Mr. Peter was an amateur carpenter and had constructed the coffins out of used playpens, lumberyard fence posts and chicken wire. The mattress was a wafer-thin piece of foam.

What you could see of the coffin room you saw through the chicken wire. The only thing missing was barbed wire and a prison tower with a search light constantly scanning the room, and with more time they might have eventually installed those things.

The ceilings were very high, but you couldn't really see very high up once you were inside your coffin for the night. The coffin room's windows were placed high on the wall and covered with thick, insulating curtains, which, Mrs. Mary would patiently explain, were very necessary for keeping us warm in that drafty old place. Since we were only in that room at night and during naps, the thick curtains were always pulled shut, and they blocked out most of the daylight and much of the streetlights that might have brightened up the creepy look of such a dungeon.

In the darkened room, the walls were colorless, though dimly lit figures would occasionally take shape on them, passing through the room as shadowy, flickering jungle animals. They remained poised and eyed the room with their bright eyes, sprung out suddenly to hunt, and then just as quickly shrank away.

Each night, after we children bathed, brushed our teeth and made our toilet, we were placed into our coffins (we never used that word in front of Mr. Peter, Mrs. Mary or the social workers who were occasionally shown around the place.) Younger children were housed two to each coffin, and this is how I first met Brian, my coffin mate.

Mr. Peter came around with his ring of keys. He stood by each child and heard us recite our bedtime prayers.

> Now I lay me down to sleep,
>
> I pray the Lord my soul to keep;
>
> if I should die before I wake,
>
> I pray for God my soul to take.

He said goodnight, smiling all the while he locked us in.
Click-click.

Brian would always say, "Good night, Papa," and "Good night, Mama." I was never fooled into calling them that because I knew my real parents were far away in San Francisco. They lived by the Golden Gate Bridge, ate as much spaghetti and saltwater taffy as they liked, and would not have forced their children to sleep in fortified, chicken-wired play pens.

I wondered if they ever thought about me or tried to find me. I could not imagine why anyone would allow things to turn out the way they did for me, for all of us. It had to be an accident, me winding up in the orphanage. I could not imagine anyone actually planning what happened to me. Or Brian for that matter.

Every night, Brian and I lay head-to-head on the same flat pillow, and as soon as Mr. Peter and Mrs. Mary left, I'd whisper to him.

"I s'pose there are bars on those windows," I'd say, squinting in the darkness to try and see what lay hidden behind the heavy curtains. Or, "I wonder where I can get some dynamite."

Brian would answer, "Dynamite? Like in cartoons?" Brian believed the Road Runner was real.

"The real stuff," I said, sure that it existed outside of cartoons.

Brian clutched his stuffed giraffe and sucked his thumb. I thought of telling him not to suck his thumb—sucking thumbs was for babies—but I needed him to stay quiet if I had any hope of getting out of there.

Brian was the smallest, youngest boy there. He was bony, his head knobby enough that you could see his lumpy scalp through his pale, blond crew cut, his face too wide and his mouth too small. But he was a real cute kid. His face really lit up when he was happy, and the funniest thing was that it did not take much to make him happy.

He didn't care at all about sleeping in a coffin. In fact, he could fall asleep anywhere, anytime. I'd once seen him limp and fast asleep on a three-legged stool in the orphanage's dining hall. He was lying on his back in a perfect arch over the stool. His head hung down on one side and his legs tangled on the other. I could see his skinny rib cage moving up and down with each breath. A giraffe pillowed his head off the dirt floor.

As long as he had his giraffe with him, he was fine, life was good.

I wished things were that simple for me.

I wondered what his real story was. Cute kid like him—why would his real parents have given him up? Looking at him in our coffin with his knobby head and his giraffe, I felt a mixture of tenderness and resentment at a world that forced such a sweet boy to live in an orphanage.

I was already hardened. I had just turned five.

"You need a key, first of all."

"A key?" he'd yawn.

"How else are we going to unlock the coffin lid and get ourselves out?"

I'd continue plotting and planning, sometimes whispering to Brian, sometimes only in my own head. Brian always fell asleep soon after we had been locked in. My mind raced long after.

One night, it was Mrs. Mary who made the rounds. Brian asked for Mr. Peter, and Mrs. Mary said, "Papa is working late."

Brian sniffled.

"Still have that nasty cold, baby?" she asked. Oh, she could sound really sweet.

She leaned close to us, and I could smell the perfumed warmth of her hair. Decent shampoo must have been her real reason for leaving the convent. I'd heard that nuns made soap out of boiled pig fat and pumice. You could smell the pigsty in a nun's head even when her hair was pushed up and out of sight in her wimples.

But Mrs. Mary no longer wore a wimple. Her hair smelled of flowers and mint, like those ribbon candies the orphans got at Christmas. Sometimes, a strand of Mrs. Mary's hair would fall next to my mouth, and I had to fight the urge to taste it. Her skin, when it brushed against me, was how I imagined the softest bed might feel—a bed I would never in my life feel, shut up as I was in that orphanage. I almost started to cry, feeling her cheek next to my inner elbow.

Her lips brushed my forehead. "Come on," she said, lifting Brian out of the coffin. "Albert—do you want to come with us? There's plenty of room for both of you in Mama and Papa's bed."

I thought as loud as I could—screaming in my own mind. Brian, don't let her fool you! Don't go in there! You will never come out alive!

"I'm fine here, Mrs. Mary," I said in a steady voice. Please, I thought, don't leave me alone in the coffin by myself.

"Are you sure?" she asked.

I nodded.

"Well, in case you change your mind, I'll leave the nightlight on."

No chance of that, I thought. You won't get me in there, even if you beg.

She carried Brian away. She had forgotten to lock the coffin.

Forgot to lock the coffin!

My chance for escape had finally come. I listened until I could no longer hear the creaking of Mrs. Mary's bedsprings. When her voice went from hushed tones to silence and Brian's sniffles had stopped, I carefully opened the coffin lid and soundlessly slipped out. As I was slowly closing the lid, I noticed Brian's giraffe. He'd gone away without it.

Mrs. Mary was cunning. Her allure overpowered three-year-olds and made them forget all about their stuffed giraffes. Who needed a stupid toy when you could be carried in those heavenly arms of hers and sleep next to her all night long?

My heart pounded. If Brian woke up without his giraffe, he'd probably sing like a canary, and I'd be discovered when she came back for it. I'd have to somehow get the giraffe to him before heading out. That stupid giraffe was the only thing in the way of my escape from that horrible children's home.

I reached over and grabbed it without a sound. I tiptoed through the hallway and toward the nightlight. When I peeped inside Mrs. Mary and Mr. Peter's room, Mrs. Mary and Brian were sound asleep.

I looked down at the giraffe under my arm and kept going, reasoning that if Brian came after me, I'd hand him the giraffe to keep him quiet. I made my way through the darkened house, fearful of every shadow. I knew Mr. Peter might be home at any moment. I'd have to hurry.

Chapter 2—Haunted

While that night of freedom gave me untold bliss, I also felt for the first time its dreadful counterbalance—a phantom pursuer that whispered and whimpered in shame, spilling out stories that burned in every word.

Its repeated moans were, at first, unintelligible from the windy voice of October, which spoke in creaks and groans through unseen trees. The phantom's voice gradually became more distinct, and once the meaning of its words began to shape, I grew alarmed.

Had I had witnessed my first ghost? Were the dead scientists, my former foster parents, speaking to me from their Peruvian mountainside graves from thousands of miles away and a good six feet under ground?

I searched my pajama pocket for the last of their soft, scientific model of the earth, the only souvenir I had from my early days in their care. I squeezed it just as I'd seen them do countless times as they worked through their quasi-theological hypothesis about the earth's origins.

They hadn't lived to complete their work. Were they coming to tell me how to carry on their project? I had always kept the small, sand-filled balloon hidden in my pocket or clutched in my fist. I sensed its possibilities in every squeeze.

The disembodied voice repeated itself, each time more loudly than the last. It punctuated each word in unearthly gasps and sobs. Truly, it was possessed, this devil. I had learned by watching countless episodes of the Twilight Zone—the scientists considered it spiritual education for me— that things always went from bad to worse in these kinds of situations.

I fled the scene.

Dead leaves fell on me and all around me. I feared the sound I made crunching them underfoot would attract Mr. Peter or the jackals and hyenas that I'd glimpsed on my shadowy bedroom walls at night. It was scary enough to be chased by ghosts, but to be torn apart by nightmare scavengers was more than a boy of five could take.

I still had Brian's giraffe under one arm and a Zorro lunchbox under the other. Before I escaped the foundling home, I'd gone to the orphanage's kitchen and quickly gathered provisions for the long exodus that lay ahead. I socked away a cylinder of Braunschweiger and as many slices of Wonder bread as I could squeeze into Zorro, filling in the remaining gaps with Cheerios. I sighed when I realized I'd have to leave the mustard bottle behind.

I filled the matching thermos with milk and considered pouring in some chocolate syrup. My escape called for new deprivations I would have to bear. Plain white milk would have to suffice.

I remembered some last essential items and wondered if I'd have enough time to grab them. I strained to hear the sound of Mr. Peter's ghost-white Plymouth Rambler in the driveway but heard nothing. I listened for Mrs. Mary. I had last seen her quietly sleeping with one of the sick orphans, Brian, in a bedroom just above the kitchen. All was quiet.

So, I scaled the cabinet and climbed onto the countertop, then reached inside the spice cupboard to find what I sought, a small box covered with a blue diamond. I shook it to be sure that it contained enough to get me through the winter. I grabbed a second and third box, just to be on the safe side then slid down.

I knew they were forbidden. But almost everything was forbidden in the orphanage. Talking with one's mouth full. Walking through the house with muddy feet. Forgetting to say "Please" and "Thank you."

These things, I knew, were the worst and most illicit of all forbidden things. And once they were in hand, I couldn't stop myself from trying just one. And then another. And then another. The rush of power from causing each tiny flame—as if I had created life itself—made me giddy.

I understood what drove the scientists to work without sleep, without food, and ultimately what drove them to leave me behind to pursue their studies in peace. Their unchecked thirst for knowledge, for discovery, eventually wound up killing them.

I jammed the matches inside the lunchbox and squeezed it shut, snapping both latches. At last, I slipped out the kitchen door and into the dark night.

Hours had gone by, and I ran as far as I could, but the wailing demon always seemed just a few steps behind me. I tripped and fell, and when I got back to my feet, I paused only long enough to grab Zorro. I scrambled away, leaving Brian's giraffe behind on the sidewalk. Maybe it would throw the demon off. Brian would never catch up even if by chance he had found a way to escape the inviting, perfumed arms of Mrs. Mary. He had always been unable to resist her charms, and his head cold made him even weaker to her than usual.

I didn't want to think about him, even though I had to admit I missed him the moment I set foot outside. I could outrun Brian, but I couldn't outrun a demon. The only sure way to lose it was to hide fast. I squeezed under the first sanctuary that presented itself, a large spruce at the end of the street where the orphanage was situated. Its needles pierced my thin pajamas, and when I began to shiver, I curled into a tight ball, praying for the night to be over.

The next thing I knew, I heard sirens. I peered through the scratchy branches of my hiding place and saw a fire truck screech around the corner then fly down my street. Another quickly followed, and then police cars and several ambulances raced by. The speeding traffic gave the fallen leaves an afterlife of chaotic, ethereal flight along the street.

One last vehicle sped past. It was a ghost-white Plymouth Rambler. In the bright lights of the emergency vehicles, I could see the horrified, flame-red expression on Mr. Peter's face. The ghost began sobbing and moaning again, closing in on me in my hiding place. I was trapped and could no longer escape the true meaning of its shrieks.

"I didn't do it!" it cried out in little boy's sobs. "I didn't do it!"

Chapter 3—Dreamed

Sharp pains sting my arms and rip across my shoulders. I am being whipped to death in punishing nightmares, guilty of unacknowledged crimes I can't remember committing.

An unseen, nighttime tormentor sits atop me like a schoolyard bully, pinning me in my narrow bed. It orders me to say the words of release, words others have long tried to put in my mouth but that I never say. My nightmare is asking me to make a full confession, to speak words so foreign that my mouth is unable to shape them.

At last, I wake after long hours of accusations. I sit up groaning, switch on my lamp, and adjust to reality the same way I always do— by making an inventory of the tokens I have carried with me all these years. My eyes focus on a stuffed toy giraffe that sits on the shelf across the room. Its unblinking eyes witnessed childhood delights and sorrows, its matted fur is crusted with long dried tears, its ears keep secret the childhood hopes and confessions it heard half a century ago.

I turn next to a small balloon filled with sand. It lies on top of an old metal lunchbox I keep on the nightstand. I trace the character stamped on its cover—Zorro posed with his cracking whip—and open its lid to see a tattered San Francisco postmark, dated October 24, 1957. I carefully lift out a baby food jar and hold it to the light, peering through the dusty gray substance coating its interior. I can no longer see what else might be inside.

I sort through the dozen other things I have carefully preserved all these years. They never change, these souvenirs from my life, but I wonder why it gets more and more difficult to recall their stories: how each object came into my possession; and more importantly, why I am so compelled to keep them with me. I return the objects to the lunchbox and set it aside.

I then examine the tokens of my nightmare—the bloody stains on my sheets; the fresh gashes on my arms and back; the bloody clumps of skin and hair caked under my fingernails. I am injuring myself in my sleep.

I stagger to the bathroom and turn on the tap full blast. I splash my face with handful after handful of icy water and dab my fresh wounds with a damp towel. There's nothing to do but look at myself in the mirror until the bleeding stops. There's nothing to do but try to remember the past. I concentrate on the happier times in my life.

* * *

The orphanage had burned to the ground, vaporized to a mound of smoking ashes. All the orphans and Mrs. Mary had perished, trapped inside. Brian, my coffin mate, was gone. I would never again see Brian's wide face, his knobby head and the way he could roll his tongue into a perfect cursive "w." I would never again hear the sound of Mrs. Mary's swishing hosiery as she walked by, smell the musky rosewater of her trailing scent, wonder at the mysteries suggested by her well-concealed but clearly ample bosom. I envied that Brian would spend eternity in Mrs. Mary's arms, charred though they may be.

At the tender age of five, I had understood the saving grace of my unique ability to deny myself pleasures when others so easily succumbed. I had survived the inferno because of it. A rescuer found me huddling under a spruce tree at the end of the street. I screamed when I saw him. His heavy clothing, fire helmet and axe gave him the appearance of a fiend. I kicked as he dragged me from under the tree. I tried to bite him, but his heavy gear protected him.

The sight of Mr. Peter and the torched remains of the foundling home snapped me out of it. Mr. Peter was sobbing into Brian's giraffe, the toy I'd dropped in my hasty attempt to run away from the home. When the fireman presented me to him, I saw that Mr. Peter's face was sooty with grief. He blinked and looked at the giraffe, then examined me again, realizing I was not that sweet boy who could roll his tongue into a double loop. His initial look of relief—even joy—drooped to disappointment. He set me down by his side and cried no more.

The lights of the emergency vehicles illuminated the horrific scene. It was immediately clear there was nothing left for the firemen to do but roll up the hoses that had hissed and spit on the flames to no avail. Ashen vapors rose from the wreckage, and I saw them shape into the ghosts of the house and all its contents—gray wisps curled into table legs where the dining room once stood, the stand and arms of a coat rack reassembled in a hovering, unnecessary afterlife; a phantom hallway mirror that glittered, catching the first light of the morning, which quickly vanished.

I immediately calculated what I might earn from conducting tours of the place. We had to do something, I reasoned, to make our living. I thought of places where I could post signs so terror tourists would know how to distinguish one pile of blackened ash from another. I approached an area where the kitchen door had opened to the yard and saw, in the yard, an empty baby food jar that had somehow survived the fire. It was the kind of thing Mrs. Mary would have saved for Mr. Peter's carpentry hobby—a small jar perfect for his tiny pieces of hardware. I opened it and crept close to the house to scoop up some ashes. A kid could make a killing selling jars of orphanage debris.

Despite my often tragic history, I had not yet felt myself cursed, even though I had barely begun my school years and had already burned through two-and-a-half sets of parents—the biological ones who literally sent me packing (via the US Postal Service); the doomed scientists who took me through toddlerhood; and now my latest stepmother, Mr. Peter's wife.

A fireman took Mr. Peter aside to show him an object he'd found under the spruce tree. It was a Zorro lunch box. He opened it, showed the contents to Mr. Peter, then pointed to me with a questioning look. Mr. Peter looked at me and nodded. The fireman called other rescue workers over, and everyone gazed into the lunchbox.

Day had arrived, and the complete destruction was even more apparent. I wanted to ask why no one was putting Mr. Peter into handcuffs for the reckless endangerment of so many orphaned children. He had, after all, kept all of us caged up. I had been the only one to escape, and just barely. I was ready to say something when I noticed the fireman turning the lunch box over and shaking out its contents. There was nothing left of the Braunschweiger, Wonder bread and Cheerios I had quickly packed before making my getaway. The thermos with its frugal measure of unflavored milk was nowhere to be found.

Only three boxes of wooden kitchen matches spilled to the ground. Everyone turned to me, talking among themselves but saying nothing I could hear. I dropped the baby food jar and felt around for the tiny, sand-filled balloon I kept in my pajama pocket, then hid it in my fist and squeezed it anxiously.

Chapter 4—Awoken

Insomnia fills the gaps between my nightmares. My two sleep disorders are like unhappily married parents staying together for the sake of the children. Their arguments feast on each other's flaws, and even when they are not talking to each other, the dark, silent house is filled with unbearable, unspoken discord.

Morning arrives and with it more proof that sleep fails me. The kaleidoscope of dawn, the racket of birds, and the alarms of garbage and bakery trucks backing up to the curb—all these lights and sounds of morning remind me of everything that I am denied. I will never be like those normal people who wake with a yawn and a stretch with spirits freshly aired by loose and fluid sleep.

* * *

That night of the fire was my first full night without sleep, but sleeplessness only sharpened my faculties. I knew that nothing good lay ahead for me, though no one said a word.

All of the adults—the firemen and Mr. Peter—had that look on their faces, the one that announces how they are superior and how you are an idiotic, uncomprehending, naive child. The adults look at you yet don't see you. They speak about you in the third person as if you are not in the room though you are, in fact, standing close by. They speak for you as if you are as inanimate as a rug.

That morning, I was being eyed and talked about but not spoken to. Nothing was explained to me, though everything they discussed was about me.

While the adults continued their discussion, I stood under a leafless ash tree on the boulevard. The sky was growing brighter, but the rising sun still lay hidden behind houses on the other side of the street. The elongated, woeful shadows of the houses fell prostrate as if in grieving, though I knew they were only pretending to be mourning the loss of their longtime neighbor. Their front yards were littered with the dead, dew-damp leaves that the trees had shed, not as tears, but like old hobbies they would lose interest in pursuing.

Finally, the sun came over the rooftops, and rays of sunlight beamed through the bare tree limbs lighting Mr. Peter in a gentle glow. He still wore his green bus driver's uniform, having arrived home in the late hours after pulling a double shift. With so many mouths to feed and no congregation to support him, he often had to work extra hours. Shepherding a flock of poor, meek, sometimes sickly and only partly sane riders through the decayed inner city was a natural role for an ex-priest.

In that light and in his uniform, with the smoke still clinging to the air, he looked holy, and I could imagine him softly speaking sermons or hearing confessions. I never knew what crime caused him to be thrown out of his church, but seeing him like that, I could understand why Mrs. Mary had chosen to follow him. She'd quietly left the convent only a few days after he'd been defrocked. But she was dead now, he no longer had so many mouths to feed, and maybe this was why he took on a pronounced mystical presence by standing on the lawn in front of the destroyed orphanage. The firemen arranged themselves around him like apostles in a church fresco. He bowed his head, spoke what appeared to be plots or prayers, then walked toward me. As soon as he arrived in front of me, I fell to my knees, longing to belong to him but still fighting the urge to be his believer.

He surprised me by gently lifting me into his arms. I surprised myself by burying my head in his shoulder. Mr. Peter carried me to the ghost-white Rambler, opened the back door and set me inside on the bench seat. I noticed an object lying next to me. It was something that had belonged of Mrs. Mary, the very last thing that she had touched—the lace chapel veil she modestly bobby-pinned to her hair every Sunday and wore to mass. Mr. Peter and Mrs. Mary had still believed, even after what the church had done to them.

A fireman opened the door and handed me the Zorro lunch box and the stuffed giraffe, giving me a look I didn't deserve, then closed the door behind him with no explanation and no apology. I opened the lunch box and placed two objects inside—the baby food jar that I'd filled with ashes and the small, sand-filled balloon. Taped inside the lunchbox lid was a San Francisco postmark dated October 24, 1957. I snapped the lid shut and set it on the floor.

I curled up on the seat next to the veil, and pressed it to my nose and inhaled deeply, then cradled it and pressed it to my lips. The small, intricately knotted piece that I knew Mrs. Mary had crocheted for herself began to calm me. My eyes began to close. Mr. Peter started the car, and he let it idle while he waited for the cigarette lighter to heat. Before it popped out, before the car had even left the driveway, I fell into a dreamless sleep, Mrs. Mary's chapel veil still pressed to my mouth.

Chapter 5—Confessed

These days, I worship only my toaster. It is my omnipotent kitchen appliance, it hears my confessions and gives me my daily bread. A dispassionate household deity, my toaster presides over my misfortunes with its awful and sometimes acrid silence. It alternates between burning and neglecting slices with no particular logic and no regard for the sanctity of my white, rye, or artisanal whole-grain bread. Occasionally, a perfectly browned specimen is delivered to me. I am mystified as to what will please it and what will cause it to blacken my morning. Though I have not believed in God for many years, I fear divine retribution from my toaster. I unplug it after every use.

As I stand in daily prayer in front of my toaster, I finger a pewter medal that hangs on a chain around my neck. The medal contains the picture of a saint, one I know almost as if he were my brother. The saint carries a club and an image of Jesus and wears a flame on his head. I've worn the medal for almost fifty years. Though I am a non-believer, the saint's image urges me to be persistent and to believe in myself despite what others say. The saint suffered because his identity was often mistaken with a traitor who had the same name.

I have lived under an assumed name my entire life, and people often thought of me as a traitor. I have never understood where I had gone wrong, why I am seen only as a daily irritation, why I am the burnt toast that curses everyone's day.

* * *

After we were left homeless by the orphanage fire, Mr. Peter and I took up residence in the ground level catechism classrooms of the Church of St. Jude, a small Catholic church situated in the river valley that formed the border of our town. The church sat on a small rise above two lonely marshes that were filled with the river's backwater in spring. In the summer, marsh grasses and waterfowl thrived there. When we arrived in November, the migrating birds had left, and the marshes were bone dry. The reedy grasses had turned brown, the trees were ashen and bare, and the place looked as deserted as a forgotten graveyard.

Every year, another house in that small, dying community fell victim to the annual floods, and another parishioner and his family moved away for good. But St. Jude's had as its namesake the patron saint of lost causes, so the church stayed even as it grew steadily emptier on Sundays. Its unfilled pews vibrated with the mournful call and response of the swing bridge and the towboats, and its confessionals heard only the wind-hushed churchyard willows and the hungry cries of birds.

It was Father Aloysius, a brother of Mr. Peter's from his days as a priest, who offered us refuge. When he first showed us around, he pointed out the discolorations that marked the cinder block walls of the classrooms like three dark bathtub rings. These were the highwater marks from the great floods of 1890, 1943 and 1955. Father Aloysius assured us that the new dike system, put in place after the 1955 flood, adequately protected the church from all but the most cataclysmic event—a 500-year flood.

Mr. Peter said that we'd had more than our share of cataclysms in the past few months, but even that did not mean there were not a few more ahead. He gave me an unreadable look, and the two men had a quiet conversation in the church kitchen, occasionally looking my way. Some decision was reached that they shook hands over, and afterward it was Father Aloysius who took the primary role for my care, spiritual and otherwise, when Mr. Peter was at work.

After a few days, Mr. Peter and I had furnished our little rooms with donations and unsold merchandise from the parish's Christmas craft sale. We covered our Boy Scout cots with crazy quilts made from linen remnants and factory seconds. We stuffed tea cozies with homemade doll clothes to create pillows. We hung a series of paint-by-number paintings of the stations of the cross on our walls. Station #6 wound up next to Mr. Peter's bed. Before he drifted off, he was treated to a vision of beautiful Veronica dabbing Christ's face with her violet cloak. My bed faced Stations #10 and #11, Jesus being stripped of his clothes and Jesus being crucified.

I outfitted myself in faded hand-me-downs, even using other boys' outgrown underwear and socks. We couldn't be choosy, Mr. Peter told me, and I really didn't mind. I was shy and not likely to ever have friends, yet I found other boys' clothes oddly comforting. I often imagined the boys who had previously owned my clothes. Boys with parents and homes and lives I would never have—lives with baseball games, movies and the occasional TV dinner. Boys who did not have to look at a badly painted images of Christ being nailed to the cross every night as they lay down to sleep. I would close my eyes and imagine myself in their homes with the sound of a cowboy show on television and the smell of Salisbury steak, foamy rehydrated potatoes, sweet corn and cherry cobbler rising from their tinfoil plates.

Mr. Peter located some work clothes for himself. He found a half dozen pairs of burnt-orange corduroys in perfect condition and multicolored flannel shirts. He even found a serviceable pair of work boots. He had volunteered his services to Father Aloysius as a groundskeeper and gravedigger at the St. Jude's cemetery in return for our rooms.

After we settled in, I saw Mr. Peter very little. When he wasn't driving his bus, he put on the corduroys, the flannel shirts, the work boots, and a terrible-looking homemade hat and scarf and set off to tend the cemetery. St. Jude's cemetery was the last resting place of Mrs. Mary, Brian, and the other orphans who died in the fire. Mr. Peter apparently preferred their quiet company to mine.

Father Aloysius was robust and seemed too cheerful for a priest. With Mr. Peter as my only model, I had thought priests were mournful and meek. But Father Aloysius spoke loudly, bellowed with laughter (and sometimes anger) and was forever slapping me hard on my shoulders when he spoke to me. I gritted my teeth when I heard him shouting for me to come to the rectory and keep him company. He insisted I call him Uncle Al, but I continued to call him Father Aloysius. He always greeted me with a ferocious embrace, and he smelled of a sweet and foreboding odor that fed my dark curiosity.

I quickly learned the daily routines of Saint Jude's. On weekday afternoons, I would find Father Aloysius passed out on a pew snoring loudly, an empty flask rising and falling on his chest. I grew bold watching him sleep and drool, and I finally got the courage to find out what was in his flask. I lifted it to smell the honeyed, pungent odor of alcohol, and shook out its few last brown drops onto my tongue. Its hot bite tingled and left me eager to try more. One day, I found him snoring in the rectory's armchair and boldly drank what I found left in the glass next to him. It was syrupy and tasted like fermented raisins and liquid brown sugar, almost like the last spoonful of my morning oatmeal but with a potent, stinging aftertaste.

One Saturday afternoon, just after the first snow, I went looking for Father Aloysius, eager to show him my first snowman. The rectory was empty, and I remembered it was the hour when he heard weekly confessions. I felt free to linger for once in his home, which was nothing more than a collection of small alcoves. Off to one side, a bedroom was tucked away behind a dark curtain. Across from it and up a small staircase was a bathroom. Along one wall there was a kitchenette with just the bare essentials—a miniature refrigerator, a sink, and a laughably child-sized stove that I knew Father Aloysius rarely used. It was spotless.

I saw a half-empty liquor bottle on the end table next to his armchair and next to it a used glass that contained a film of the liquid I had been sampling. I opened the bottle and poured myself half a glass more. I glanced behind me, saw I was still alone, then drank it down quickly, delighted by the sensation of it lighting my throat on fire. I felt a tingling sensation down my legs. I grew warm. I poured another half glass, emptying the bottle, and then gulped it down. I sat in his chair while I felt strange sensations wash over me, and I wondered if what I was feeling was the warm grace of God. Was I being blessed at last?

I made my way into the church and immediately tripped on the kneelers in front of the altar, falling hard to my knees. I looked at the cross and squinted to see the thorns pressed against Jesus's head, his trickling blood wavering in front of my eyes as if he had just died in front of me. My eyes began to hurt. I crawled to the confessional and entered.

As soon as I leaned on the kneeler, the confessional window slid open. Father Aloysius's face was obscured by the dark screen, and I wondered if he knew it was me on the other side.

"Are you here to confess?" he asked. His voice sounded forgiving yet I remained silent. I heard the distinctive heavy creak of foyer doors being opened at the church's entrance, and I knew another sinner was entering the church. I slipped out of the confessional and hurried to the sanctuary door. The new sinner entered the confessional, and I heard the moan of the kneeler, then the steady whisper of secrets.

I knew it was only a matter of time before the absolved confessor would exit and locate the nearest pew to mumble his penance—a dozen Hail Marys and Our Fathers, perhaps. If he'd been truly bad, an entire rosary or two. I hid in the shadows by the side entrance sinking to the floor. I noticed something small and round, about the size of a coin, on the floor next to me. It was a medal bearing the image of St. Jude, the patron saint of the church. I remembered the prayer Father Aloysius had been teaching me, St. Jude's prayer, the prayer for forgotten causes:

Faithful servant and friend of Jesus, the name of traitor has caused you to be forgotten by many, but the true Church invokes you universally as the patron of things despaired of. Pray for me that finally I may receive the consolations and the succor of Heaven in all my suffering.

Like St. Jude, I was living proof of the cost of mistaken identity, for hadn't I been mistaken for a criminal? Hadn't my own parents forgotten me, and my many sets of foster parents as well? I clutched the medal in my hand and waited quietly until my head cleared and the sinner left the church.

Father Aloysius finished hearing confessions and retired to the rectory to prepare for the Sunday homily. Soon after, I went down to the classroom and slid the Zorro lunchbox from its hiding place under my Boy Scout cot. The paint-by-number Jesus watched from his crucifix as I opened the lid and dropped the St. Jude medal inside. St. Jude had never cleared his name, the name he shared with the traitor, Judas Iscariot.

I might never either.

Chapter 6—Burned

Despite his profession, Father Aloysius proved himself completely uninterested in guiding me spiritually or otherwise. In fact, he sought me out. He was desperate for company in his lonely parish. Father Aloysius loved to play cards, and he had no one to indulge his love of gambling, so he taught me how to play poker, keeping me with him long after I should have been in bed. Night after night, we sat at his kitchen table and played poker, making our wagers with macaroni noodles and grains of Uncle Ben's converted rice.

When Mr. Peter learned about my late evenings with Father Aloysius, I begged to be put into school. He agreed, made arrangements, and found a way to explain to Father Aloysius that I needed to be in my bedroom after dinner because I had chores to do. Mr. Peter had me shine his bus driver shoes. He'd again taken up woodworking and made a small shoe-shine box out of scrapped lumber and outfitted it with rags and polish. Every night, I would work the polish into his shoes, even when they were still warm from a day of wear, and not quit until I could see my face darkly reflected in each one. When I had finished, I set his shoes by Station #14 where Jesus is laid in his tomb and covered with incense.

Though my card playing days ended, Mr. Peter insisted I attend to another service for Father Aloysius. I was to be his altar boy and carry the thurible, the metal container for burning holy incense. Father Aloysius would instruct me in this solemn duty in time for the feast of Christmas mass.

The first day I went to the sanctuary for my training, Father Aloysius's bloodshot eyes lit up on seeing me and for once his face wore a thoughtful expression. He didn't greet me with a heavy slap across the shoulder, nor did he talk so loudly it made my ears ring. Instead, he quietly gestured for me to approach the small cabinet where the chalices, bowls and other valuable and holy items used during mass were locked away.

He removed the thurible from its silk-lined case and held it out gently as if it were a newborn baby. It was a shiny brass bowl suspended from chains with a cone-shaped lid. He explained how the boat, a dish with a hollow chamber and spoon, was used to hold the incense, and then he showed me a box that contained granules of frankincense and myrrh. I smelled the exotic and earthy scent, and it filled me with anxiety. The heavy, oily odor required a devotion and focus that I wasn't prepared to give. Father Aloysius didn't seem to notice my doubt. And so, my training began.

As he explained the process to me, it was more complicated than I would have ever imagined. Before mass, I was to collect the charcoal, fire starter, lighter, incense, thurible and boat, and take these items outside, where I would light the fire starter and put coals on the rack above the flames to heat them. I had to have the thurible ready to use at Christmas mass during the initial procession, the Gospel reading during communion, and at the recession at the end of mass. Each time I had to put the incense into the boat, place coals flat in the thurible, then properly vent the lid so that the coals would remain hot and the incense would heat and burn properly.

I wonder how much Father Aloysius knew, or remembered, of what he'd been told about the demise of the orphanage. It seemed odd that Mr. Peter would allow me to have anything to do with fire considering that a fire had taken away everyone we held dear. Shouldn't he have mentioned how traumatic this could be to me? Carrying around a smoky orb, one that emitted incense that was used to bless the dead? Perhaps he wanted me to atone for sins that he thought I'd committed. Perhaps he hoped the exercise would make me suffer for Mrs. Mary's loss.

I knew I should be angry with him for forcing me to take on this service for the church. I thought again about packing everything up and running away like I had from the orphanage. But there was nowhere to go. I was even less familiar with the area around St. Jude's than I was with the orphanage's neighborhood. Every day was colder and darker then the previous one. It snowed every day without stopping. I was already living in a place of sanctuary. Who else would take me in?

December arrived and I still didn't have the coals properly heating before we had to move on to the actual procession into church, which involved a lot of kneeling, bowing, swinging and circling. Half the time, I left the incense boat outside, forgetting to carry it in with the thurible when I came around to the church. I was forever on the wrong side of Father Aloysius. My open area swings were too small. When I was in more confined spaces, I wound up hitting something. But Father Aloysius believed I could learn. In fact, he was the first person who had ever believed in me at all. I hoped I wouldn't disappoint him, but I knew he would eventually be disappointed in me. So far, everyone had been.

Father Aloysius was a master at swinging the censor. In his hand, the thurible moved smoothly and always on course. The incense formed smoky curlicues that blessed the air but didn't leave an impenetrable fog. Father Aloysius had a way of making the incense take on the shape and being of that third, mystical person of the Holy Trinity—the Holy Ghost. As the incense filled the air, the misty arms of God reached out to wrap around the true believers. I waited to be embraced by the warm fragrance but found myself often having to fight off coughing attacks. The smoke choked me.

Still, the sight of Father Aloysius with the censor was a miracle in my eyes. I loved watching that big, fat man move with grace, assurance, and dignity—a man who, in every other area of his life, was a loud, drunken lout. Witnessing Father Aloysius at his best, as he was during the communion blessings, with his firm command of the censor, made the 300-pound man look like he had the agility and tenderness of a ballet dancer in a pas de deux. I can still see Father Aloysius on his knees during the blessing of the Eucharist raising the thurible high and censing deftly on each beat.

Holy, holy, holy Lord, God of power and might
Do this for the remembrance of me (bread)
Do this for the remembrance of me (wine)
…in the unity of the Holy Spirit all honor and glory is yours, Almighty Father, now and forever, AMEN

I watched without breathing (it helped me to stave off the coughs) and in complete amazement, transfixed by the display. If there had been a hall of fame for thurible waving, he'd have been in it.

But Christmas was a week away and I still was not even at amateur level in my ability to keep the coals lit. The fourth Station of the Cross—Jesus meeting his mother—hung next to the sink where I brushed my teeth at night. Jesus, of course, had greater sorrows than trying to keep a few coals lit, but he had Mary at his side in his darkest hours. I had no one. The Mary in my life was gone. I had no mother, not even a temporary one. I couldn't bear to look at the badly painted picture of the two of them together—Jesus with blood pouring down and Mary with her gracious, sorrowful tears—so I took it down, folded the flimsy cardboard painting in half and hid it at the bottom of the Zorro lunchbox. I held the St. Jude medal in my hand and wondered if even St. Jude could help such a lost cause as me.

Chapter 7—Resurrected

I don't celebrate any holidays, particularly not Christmas. With no living family and a social circle that has dwindled over the years—though to be honest was never particularly robust—I really have no one to celebrate.

I am, by nature, a social person and I have a scientific bent, am very well read and articulate. These harmonious personal characteristics would bring people flocking to me if I were any other person. My history as Albert Park has proven just the opposite. People run away from me. As a result, I have little chance to practice one of my unique scientific talents—physiognomy.

My interest in this branch of science dates from an early age when I could stare for hours at classmates, teachers, and anyone, so fascinated was I to unlock the secrets told by their faces. I am still astonished that advanced degrees are not offered in such an important field. My advanced level of independent study has made me a genius in understanding peoples' characters based on a quick study of their faces.

Some faces tell beautiful stories, but these are rare. Many would say that children's faces, unblemished by denials, are the most beautiful, but they are, of course, unappealing to those who are learned in the field of physiognomy. The science is most interested in close study of faces that are crooked with treachery and gnarled with deceit. I can tell you every sin a person has committed, or will commit, from the way a hair grows from their ears. Moles are particularly telling.

This gift I have for reading faces may have contributed to the end of many budding friendships, romances and business dealings. I feel driven to reveal to people what is foretold in their wrinkles, freckles, and scars, and how heeding my words can avert their suffering. Yet—and to this day—I am completely taken aback by this. People always take offense, even when what I tell them is the plain truth visible on their own faces.

Just this morning, for instance, a gentleman who rode my bus quickly caught my attention. His face was a marvel of distortions, and I was ready to study him closely. He sat across from me on a bank of seats directly behind the bus driver. I noticed how heavily freckled his pale face was. The freckles were patterned as distinctly as snowflakes. He gave me a disturbed look as I continued to study the warped folds of his neck and a small protrusion on the crooked bridge of his nose. I knew these foretold many disasters, most involving money, and I wanted to caution him not to speculate in the stock market. I was about to tell him this when he gave me a disturbing look, stood up, and relocated to the back of the bus muttering "asshole" as he got away.

People do not want to hear the truth. Mr. Peter didn't want to tell the truth about himself. Whether Father Aloysius ever faced up to his truth, I never knew. I never saw him again after my first Christmas with him so many years ago.

* * *

Christmas morning had arrived and began the same as any other morning at St. Jude's. Mr. Peter was up, dressed, and off to the cemetery to visit the graves of Mrs. Mary and Brian, bringing with him fresh evergreen wreathes to ornament their gravestones.

When I woke, I noticed a few small packages by my bed. There were shiny new shoes to wear to mass, a child's collection of Bible stories, and a small, handmade, wooden car that clearly had come from Mr. Peter's workshop. It was in the exact image of the ghost-white Rambler with doors that opened and small removable figures of a boy and a man inside.

I had to marvel at Mr. Peter's workmanship. I knew enough already not to believe in Santa Claus.

Father Aloysius invited me to have breakfast with him in the rectory and managed to provide me with a cup of cocoa and perfectly toasted bread and jam. He had the same meal, though I noticed he poured a small bottle a shot or two into his cocoa. I smelled a minty aroma and asked for some in my cup. Father Aloysius turned red and explained that those spirits were intended for clergy only.

We prepared for mass, and I have to say that even Father Aloysius was pleasantly surprised to see how well I was handling my altar boy duties. The coals were heating perfectly, I had the proper amount of incense in the boat, and I was carrying the thurible with authority at the precise time required. Mr. Peter even smiled when he saw me in my altar boy robe standing at Father Aloysius' side ready to proceed into the church.

The church pews were packed. Everyone connected to St. Jude had come home to attend the Christmas services. Small girls in velvet coats of jeweled hues—sapphire, emerald and ruby—stood by their beautifully coiffed, elegantly dressed mothers. Young boys matched their suited, polished fathers with cheeks glowing red from the heat of so many bodies together. A hand occasionally drifted down to smooth some child's errant hairs. Restless little boys yanked at the unaccustomed tightness of their collars. Toddler feet tapped their shiny, patent leather shoes on the hard wooden pews. New mothers rocked swaddled infants, all of whom, miraculously, seemed placid. The choir sang Christmas hymns of thanks and praise. I felt as peaceful and pure as if I had just been born. The wonder of Christmas morning rang through me with its joyous song. At Father Aloysius' side, I had found my place in the world, and everyone looked on approvingly.

Every aspect of the service went as perfectly as the initial procession. When incense was required at the Gospel reading and during communion, I was on cue. The curlicues of scented smoke lifted in time with each prayer, and I felt exhilarated in the perfumed forgiveness of the air.

The flawless performance continued and only the recessional was left. Though I was somewhat nauseous from the heavy smell in the air, I was once again prepared and standing next to Father Aloysius as he spoke the closing prayers. I waited by his side at the foot of the altar with sunlight streaming through the sanctuary's stained-glass windows and lighting the aisle. Suddenly, Father Aloysius stepped forward and raised the thurible, censing the way ahead of us. The drifting smoke took on gorgeous tints in the prismatic light, flickering in a dizzying display.

The faces watching from the pews began to waver, blur, then finally vanish. In the center of the aisle, other forms took shape, coalescing into two figures. Mrs. Mary appeared with Brian at her side. Both wore shimmering holiday clothes that flickered as if lit by Christmas lights. They waited next to a pew where Mr. Peter stood with his head respectfully bowed.

What happened next, I was told later, but have never believed it. People claimed I screamed as if possessed. I condemned everyone in the church, spitting the horrid details of each person's individual doom. I used coarse language that was wholly inappropriate for a church and certainly unexpected from a young boy. Mr. Peter dragged me down the aisle and out the door, but I tore away to run back inside and make the most disgusting accusations against Father Aloysius. I kicked Mr. Peter as he struggled at last to carry me away.

I don't understand how that terrible fantasy of Christmas was used against me, or why the real truth had to be covered up.

Here is what I know happened.

Mrs. Mary and Brian came to deliver a message on Christmas. I think Brian wanted me to know how happy he was that I was taking care of his giraffe and was stopping by for a visit. Mrs. Mary held out her arms and beckoned me to hurry along because it was time for Christmas brunch. She wore her chapel veil bobby-pinned to her curly brown hair. The incense in the air reminded me of her perfume. I may have been carried away in my joy of seeing them alive, and I may even have shrieked in surprise. I possibly may have wailed in grief when I reached out for their embrace and grasped nothing but incensed spirits wafting in the air. But I know I would not have used language unbecoming to a St. Jude's altar boy. Even in my youth, I prided myself on my propriety and ability to control my manners. I was not a wild, unbridled child, prone to tantrums and poor manners. Quite the opposite.

The accusations I was heard to have made against Father Aloysius were enough to have him immediately sent away from St. Jude's. He was reassigned to some parish far away in the north country. No one ever heard from him again. Priests were in such short supply that no one was available to take over for Father Aloysius. The Church of St. Jude already had a tenuous hold on its parishioners, so with Father Aloysius's departure, it completely collapsed. Masses were never held there again. I don't remember anything else of that Christmas Day. After mass, I came down with a fever and spent the rest of that day in bed, and many days after. I finally began to feel well as the New Year approached.

I woke up late on New Year's Eve and the dim room came into focus slowly. A chair was pulled close to my bed, and Mr. Peter's glasses were lying on a small side table next to his pocketknife and a small pile of wood shavings. Mr. Peter was nowhere to be seen, but on his chair he'd left the newly painted wooden car he had made me for Christmas. I could see that he'd made a couple of modifications. The tailgate now opened and closed. I peered inside it and saw he'd added more figures. Two boys now sat in the back seat, and a woman rode next to the driver. Four suitcases sat on the luggage rack on top of the car.

I couldn't resist opening the door and taking the smaller boy out. I held the perfectly carved figure in my hand, touching the smooth and carefully shaped piece. I ran a finger over the wooden boy's scalp and detected small knobby lumps that seemed familiar. I sat him on my finger and looked closely to see he had a tiny toy giraffe on his lap.

Chapter 8—Buried

Seasons, then years come and go like passengers coming and going from my bus. The scene and people change and I remain the same observant constant. Each day I sit on the same bench in my classic corduroy sports jacket, button-down shirt, jeans and laced work boots. I wear a sturdy, all-weather fedora, removing it at appropriate times. My daily needs are simple, and most are met by what I carry in my leather satchel—an umbrella, a wooden case of pencils, a paring knife, three spiral notebooks, a set of flatware, a linen napkin and a dinner plate.

I abhor the transitory, the impermanent. Such waste is particularly manifested in Styrofoam plates, paper napkins, plastic cutlery and love relationships. Of these, only the last is somewhat inescapable. One must conduct life's romantic transactions, and while I have begun every new relationship with hope and modest expectations, my affairs rarely last more than a season. There are one or two notable exceptions, but even those ended when I was unfairly found deficient.

I have learned it's always best to avoid disposables, such as paper products and girlfriends, so I don't dwell on thoughts of lost loves. I find yesterday's lunch far more memorable. I dine out alone on my own plate using my own silverware and linen napkin. Sustained in this way, I continue to live honorably and humbly with neither delusions nor hopes.

I remain in public, a pilgrim of selflessness, a paragon of altruism, while people go on ignoring my perfect example of a simple man living a moral and just life. I've come to believe that my very existence is threatening to others, as if I were a poised paring knife, ready to peel away their unexamined skins, slice and quarter their transgressions, and core their fantasies. I have yet to meet the man or woman who has the courage that is constantly required of me. I have gone under honesty's knife countless times and have many scars to prove it.

And so, the seasons come and go, the years too, and the people come and go from my life, always demanding that I change, come clean, confess. Yet it is just the opposite that is needed. This is my life's burden.

* * *

Mr. Peter and I continued to live in the Church of St. Jude even though it no longer held masses or any other religious events and though the cemetery was still accepting customers. The diocese now paid Mr. Peter to caretake the church buildings and the cemetery. In return, we were offered the rectory as an apartment and free cemetery plots.

I attended school, and because I was a prodigy, I was placed in a special class with two other children who had unique abilities not unlike my own, though I failed to see what their particular gifts were. My classmates were a pair of hyperactive twins, Robert and Roger. Robert's head was misshapen because he had tipped over swinging once and banged the back of his head on concrete. When he had a fresh crew cut, you could see a jagged scar across the back of his scalp. You could tell his brother Roger was trouble by his one-sided smile. His crooked grin could have made him a fortune modeling for jack-o-lantern carvers, if there was such a profession.

The three of us were kept in a special classroom just outside the principal's office. The twins were kept on opposite sides of the room due to their constant need to dominate everyone and everything, a quirk of their giftedness. I was stuck in the middle, and as usual, though I was blameless, I was again placed in a position where I had to defend myself against unjust claims. Just to survive, I had to be constantly wary and battle alongside these classmates in their daily competitions—who could jump the highest, spit the farthest, cause the girls to scream the loudest. It was exhausting.

Many times, Mr. Peter was called in at the end of the day so we could meet Robert and Roger and their parents for a "discussion" in the principal's office. With two troublemakers against one of me, I rarely prevailed. Routinely, I was given extra assignments at both school and home, which I completed satisfactorily and quickly, even though these punishments were unjust. To add to my indignation, I was often required to repeat school assignments I'd finished because Robert and Roger had stolen my work and then signed my name to their shoddy, stained worksheets. This meant I got their bad grades.

After a few years under Robert and Roger's domination, I finally came up with a foolproof plan to beat them for good. During third grade, Robert and Roger worked on a project that took almost the entire school year. They were constructing an escape tunnel under the playground fence, and they threatened to kill me if I told anyone. They also threatened to kill me if I didn't do their bidding and dig the tunnel for them. Since I had been their slave for years, and it was easy for the two of them to gang up on me, there was simply no use fighting them. So, I did all the digging while they kept watch. My reward was they let me eat the lunch Mr. Peter had packed for me. It was bologna, and they hated bologna.

I actually didn't mind the work. They left me alone for half an hour each day, and I liked sitting underground in the dirt. I imagined this was what things were like for Brian, who I imagined had burrowed out of his casket had a fancy little tunnel all to himself. I carried on conversations with him—asked how he liked being dead, and how Mrs. Mary was holding up. I told him some jokes I'd heard and let him know his giraffe was just fine.

The ground under the fence was sandy, so digging was easy. We reinforced the walls with whatever we could find. There were many places where I knew the walls could go at any time. What Roger and Robert didn't know was that I'd secretly made an opening above the tunnel that

I kept covered with branches. Near the secret opening, I'd been building up a good-sized pile of dirt on a large piece of cardboard. Elsewhere, I had kept a big piece of plywood hidden under a pile of leaves.

Finally, after what seemed to be weeks of heavy work, my plan went into high gear. I whispered to Robert and Roger near the tunnel's entrance, telling them that I was close to breaking through on the other side. They shoved me out of the way and squeezed in. I executed my plan as fast as I could, grabbing the plywood and covering the main entrance, then blocking it with some heavy stones. Through the secret opening, I dropped my load of dirt right on top of them and shoveled more in as fast as I could. Then, I stood on top of a poorly reinforced part of the tunnel and jumped as hard as I could. Before I knew it, the earth caved in below me. The recess bell rang, and I ran breathlessly inside.

Our current teacher's aide arrived from lunch and immediately asked if I knew where the twins were. I told her they had been on the playground and then disappeared. She raced to the principal's office and before long police cars and ambulances were screeching into the school parking lot. One police car carried a pair of German Shepherds. I could hear the dogs barking excitedly from the cars. Another squad careened into the parking lot, and I saw the twins' mother shoot out of it and hand over shirts I had seen the boys wearing. The dogs were given a whiff pf the boys' scents through the car window, then the door was opened and the dogs leaped out.

The muscular dogs circled and crisscrossed the playground, their noses stirring the dirt and scattering the footprints. Then they hurried off in one direction, slowed down over particular areas, and responded to whistles when they were ordered to head in other directions. They seemed confused by so many smells. Roger and Robert had obviously been everywhere on the playground.

The principal came for me and again asked what I knew. I owed my captors nothing, but I honestly answered, saying there was nothing to tell. I mentioned the twins had threatened me if I said anything about their activities. I asked if we were going to be sent home early.

The dogs began digging frantically by the plywood door and police and emergency personnel rushed to the site of their activity. The twins' mother ran across the playground to the tunnel's entrance, and in moments, all the adults were on the ground next to the dogs, digging as fast as they could.

Roger was pulled out first, then Robert. They hadn't suffered much more than a few anxious moments, and a light scolding from their parents, but they were given a hero's reception as if they had risen from the dead. On the other hand, I was expelled. Mr. Peter came for me, but before we left, he had a long, closed-door discussion with the principal. I was brought in as that conversation ended and the principal sat me down to say how disappointed he was in me for burying my friends alive, leaving them to die and then telling no one about it. I stammered that they had forced me to dig their tunnel, but my explanations were quashed.

The principal said, "I think WE know the truth, Albert Park." He looked at Mr. Peter as he spoke, and though I did not see Mr. Peter's face, I knew that Mr. Peter had defended me. Why, after all, would he say nothing more to me on the drive home unless he'd done just that? I saw all the children watching us in Mr. Peter's car as the buses exited the school grounds. We were the last to leave.

I glanced at Mr. Peter on the drive home and saw that his eyes were fixed on the road ahead, his face serious as always, his bus driver's cap still tight over his frizzy blond hair.

That evening, Mr. Peter explained that the principal had made it clear the school was not equipped to handle someone of my ilk. But it didn't matter anyway since the school year was ending. Summer vacation would begin a little early for me. If there was a plan for the next school year, it wasn't going to be discussed while the cave-in accusations were still fresh in everyone's minds.

I didn't care if I ever went back. I could learn on my own what I needed. I didn't need to be educated. I was a prodigy. The world needed to know more about me than I had already learned about it.

Chapter 9—Drowned

My bus doesn't take me all the way to my destination, so I have a short, difficult climb to reach my target. Of course, no vehicle could make the ascent. From where the bus stops, I scale a gravel path that winds along a steep hillside. It's arduous, but I still have my health, even though I've cut back on my daily exercise after my knees wore down due to years of hard running.

I begin my climb up the trail. Millions of years earlier, a shallow, tropical sea covered the area. More recently, mining had exposed sedimentary rock layers of Galena limestone and gray Decorah shale. As a result, the steep slopes are studded with the fossilized marine organisms that lived long ago on the ancient ocean floors. Coral-like animals, tiny clams, and ancient sea lilies entombed there for 500 million years regularly surface after each spring thaw and every rain. On my daily walks from my bus stop, I routinely come across newly emerged fossils. I leave the poor things where they are and feel uncomfortable walking on this antediluvian graveyard, but my journey requires me to travel through it, though I regret the indignity of my shoes crunching on these stone-hardened bones.

The earth routinely exposes its true history without regrets or remorse. It forgets nothing in revealing itself completely, opening as simply as a flower, as if it could not keep even the tiniest secret. I admire its abandon and have always aimed for the same level of disclosure. I do not believe that I've missed the mark by much, but I have lingering concerns. Perhaps there are layers to the truth, each as genuine as the last, but each unique. This thought might ease my burden, as well as others' doubts about what I have professed.

It would help me if there was some similar process that would aid me in unlocking what remains bottled up inside me. My process of recovery has not been gentle, nor has it helped me to find what I, and others, seek. There are moments when I sense the skeletal remains of some truth, but find it repressed by an errant, forgetful footfall. Try as I might to reconstruct my early history from a handful of fragments, I am as yet without success. This is why I must continue making my daily journey to this particular hillside, subjecting myself to whatever trauma it brings to the surface. I must force myself to uncover what lies hidden within the graveyard of memory.

* * *

Another imposed sojourn interrupted my place in a world most children take for granted. I became an elementary school exile. I did not think of myself as a dropout. I knew Mr. Peter did not either. If he had, he would not have assigned me chores that could only be handled by someone as responsible as me. While he was away at work, or on duty at the cemetery, he had me keep watch over the small garden he'd planted just outside the rectory door. I was to keep the garden free from pests, such as the hungry rabbits that seemed particularly abundant that summer. This task required I spend the entire day outdoors. He locked the church when he left, leaving a key with our closest neighbor, the mailman's widow.

Mrs. McCauley lived alone in one of the last houses in the neighborhood around St. Jude. Her house was sided in black and gray checked asphalt tiles, which gave it a grim, plaid appearance, much like an archaic board game people no longer want to play. I had my lunch with her every day in her small, grapevine-choked backyard gazebo.

Mrs. McCauley was unlike any other woman I had encountered. For one thing, she was the oldest person I had ever known. Mr. Peter

50

told me she was over one hundred, but she acted like she was sixty. Her sturdy build gave her the appearance of height. Her heavy-busted, short-waisted frame and the gray bun of hair perched on top of her head made her look like one of the tall, thick gas pumps at the Mobil station. Her appearance was accentuated by the long, heavy skirts she wore, made of the kind of cloth used in circus tents, and I guessed it would take an elephant to haul her down. The truth was, though, that she really was no giant. Her mercurial moods and outlandish ideas were what made her oversized.

She scolded me constantly for letting the gazebo screen door slam, for not finishing my milk, for leaning my bicycle against her shabby chicken wire fence. She involved me in impossible chores, such as scraping away the thick lichen that grew on the asphalt siding of her house or having me whitewash the fieldstones that lined her unused driveway.

Depending upon her disposition, she would feed chipmunks by hand, affectionately calling them "Precious" or "Semi-Precious" and cooing to them when they arrived on her porch for handouts. Later, I would come upon her disposing of dead chipmunks she had trapped inside her garden shed and complaining that they'd eaten all her seeds.

I didn't relish what she made for me, but I quickly learned that my complaints might earn me a slap on the ear. She baked her own bread, and it was often without any flavor, the crusts so hard I thought I might break my teeth tearing into them. She forced me to drink curdled, sour milk that had sat out on her counter. She made me sit with her through unending games of solitaire and required me to wash her greasy dishes before I was allowed to go home. I mowed her lawn with her ancient push-mower, though the blades were so dull the grass often simply bent to get out of the way. No matter—she had me run the mower around in the opposite direction. But Mr. Peter insisted I treat her with respect, and I knew she reported everything to him when he came by to fetch the church keys every day.

In late June, we were deluged by weeks of rain. Our garden washed away, and with the rain still gushing down, we would have to wait to replant. With nothing for me to do at the church, Mr. Peter arranged for me to stay longer with Mrs. McCauley.

Mrs. McCauley's garden was devastated, but not completely lost, so she insisted on me helping her bail it out. Both of us worked hard for a couple days at that task, bailing as fast as we could even in the pouring rain. Every night, I went home completely soaked. By the next day, my shoes still weren't dry, and with the rain continuing, there was no chance they were going to dry out anytime soon. I gave up wearing them.

When the rain continued and bailing Mrs. McCauley's garden didn't help, she set both of us to work on removing as many of the seedlings as we could and temporarily placing them in any bucket or dish she could find. She had decided to relocate her garden to a small patch of ground she owned on top of the hill, thinking the conditions might be better higher up and off the flood plain. So, we ladled out all her tomatoes, peppers, cucumbers, squash, strawberries and beans, handful by muddy handful. The radishes and onions were left where they were. Mrs. McCauley figured they'd come back on their own.

Mrs. McCauley laid claim to a rowboat that had floated up from the flooded boatyard, and we placed all of the recovered plants inside it. She christened the boat McCauley's Ark, covered it with a tarp she'd made from her old skirts, and tied it to the boulevard Dutch elm tree. The next morning, we were going to set off for higher ground, float the boat as far down the flooded roadway as we could go, then turn off where the brickyard trail led up the hill. We'd have to take trip after trip up the hill with the seedlings and carry them all to the promised land at the top. I thought of sailing home by myself in her boat, but knew it was pointless. She'd find me in an instant.

That night before the planned relocation of Mrs. McCauley's garden, Mr. Peter worked late. The floods had caused all sorts of delays on his bus route and caused mechanical problems for some of the fleet. He picked up a double shift and called Mrs. McCauley to ask if I could spend the night. She complained but agreed, considering that we'd be able to start earlier the next day and have a better chance of salvaging her vegetables.

I thought nothing of staying away from home for the night. I didn't really consider the St. Jude's rectory my home, nor the orphanage before it, nor the scientists' apartment. Still, when I laid down on Mrs. McCauley's ancient davenport in my bedroom for that night—which was her porch—and listened to the rain hitting the corrugated metal porch roof, I wondered whether I would ever fall asleep. I missed the small objects I'd kept with me. They were the only stabilizing constants from my life—Brian's stuffed giraffe, all the things in the Zorro lunchbox, in particular Mrs. Mary's chapel veil. I felt haunted without them. I thought of leaving Mrs. McCauley's and going back to the rectory for the night, but with the streets so flooded and the rain still coming down, I knew the most likely outcome of doing that would be drowning.

I even thought of going inside Mrs. McCauley's house and finding another place I could lie down and sleep, but I knew I'd be wandering through it like a ghost. I might startle her, and I did not want to come across Mrs. McCauley in her nightgown. A hundred-year-old gas pump in a negligee? I shivered. But I didn't belong on her porch. I didn't belong anywhere. I felt pained, lying there awake and listening to the rain for hours, tossing on her lumpy, musty davenport.

Before I knew it, Mrs. McCauley was sitting next to me on the couch, roughly shaking me awake. It was still dark outside. She asked whether I always had such nightmares, told me I had been shrieking. "I suppose you're homesick," she said without any tenderness. Clearly, I was causing her to lose sleep.

She went inside and turned on a lamp. I heard her rattling around in a side table drawer. I watched her shuffle back—she was not wearing a negligee but was in a ratty old plaid coat that looked like it belonged to a man, maybe Mr. McCauley.

"Here," she said in her hardened manner. "Take this."

She handed me a polished lump of a stone. In that dim light coming through her picture window, I saw the curving red and caramel bands of a small agate.

She told me that Mr. McCauley used to comb the shores of a great lake far to the north, and he would come home with buckets of stones he'd polish in a rock tumbler for days until they glowed. Some were so smoothed by the process they became transparent.

"Imagine," she said, "a rock you can see through." She croaked out a small laugh.

When her husband had died, she'd dropped all the agates into the river except for the one she handed me.

"Now lie down," she told me. "Hold that stone between your fingers and don't drop it. I heard," she mumbled, clearing her throat, "that it can help keep the bad dreams away, holding an agate in just that way." She left me then, heading back inside and shutting off the lamp.

I did as she told me. There was no point arguing with Mrs. McCauley. I lay down and held the smooth stone between my thumb and forefinger, stroked its glassy surface and sensed the many untold stories layered into its hardened minerals. I had not yet understood how unpolished I remained, despite all the abrading, fracturing and tumbling I'd experienced. I knew the possibilities the finished stone suggested, but I wanted an easier path to such brilliance. I too would be as valued and cherished as a gemstone but without the tortuous and crushing penalty it had suffered to gain its opulent exterior. I would not be held to the dictates of the pounding responsibility or grinding guilt. I would insist on having my way.

I fell asleep with Mr. McCauley's last stone in my hand.

Chapter 10—Engraved

I arrive at the top of the hill and rest at the graveyard entrance. I'm not fond of cemeteries, particularly not this one, but I come here because I'm legally required. It's a condition of my parole. I won't go into the circumstances of the charges that Albert Park was found guilty of. That, indeed, is my only comfort—that it was Albert Park who was found guilty. I have nothing I share with that man except his name, which I have gone by, it is true, since shortly after my birth. But that is a circumstance of my life, not a fact. Unfortunately, this mistaken identity has ruled my life

To be honest, like every person, my memories grow hazy as the years go by. So why does any of it matter—the quarrels, the crimes, the heartbreak—when an entire life gets summed up in deeply engraved letters and dates on a tombstone? The rest is forgotten. Humans are, in fact, forgettable. I cite this evidence—time itself considers nothing at all of our biological remains and allows the earth to reabsorb us and repeat our errors with another generation of fallible, inept, incomplete specimens. Nothing changes, and we go on telling and retelling our history, making our excuses, blaming others for our errors.

I am legally required to read for you the inscription on tombstone 26-A, and that is the only reason I stand before it now. While I object to my punishment—which seems completely arbitrary and ridiculous—I am, in fact, a law-abiding citizen, and even a simpleton can easily conclude that I am given the number of lawsuits I have filed, the majority of which have been dismissed. I sue to make the point that I believe in the law, much like the faithful regularly attend mass to prove they believe in God.

Thus, while I continue to protest my sentence, I carry it out and accept that I must continue to do so because my appeals have been exhausted. Even the high court no longer accepts any new casework submitted by Albert Park, Esquire.

I stand near a semi-circle of columnar junipers that are pruned so they spiral in whirling, heavenward corkscrews. Before me there is a small monument (numbered 26-A) engraved with the names of three people, only one of whom remains alive. I am legally bound to tell you who lies buried here.

They are:

Mary, Sweet Wife and Dear Mother

Brian, Beloved Son

* * *

When Mrs. McCauley woke me the next morning, I looked outside to see that the rain had finally let up. The streets were still flooded, but I could see that McCauley's Ark had not floated away. The tarp was still secure. The sky was filled with thick clouds that hung down like dark, full udders, but I could see a horizon blooming across the river. Mrs. McCauley was not sure if we could trust that this meant the rain had ended at last, but she wanted us to be off quickly lest it began again. I hurried to dress and eat. Mrs. McCauley pulled on a pair of Mr. McCauley's old hip waders—boots he had used when he went agate hunting in the big, cold lake up north.

Mrs. McCauley fed me a bowl of congealed oatmeal that she softened with warm milk and sweetened with honey. She sprinkled on a handful of hardened raisins. It tasted like paste, but I didn't complain. I swallowed hard and knew it would sustain me for the difficult work that was ahead.

We were ready. She removed a portion of the tarp, had me climb inside the boat, then lashed a rope to the bow. We were off, Mrs. McCauley walking along the curb and pulling the boat through the streets. When the water grew too deep on the lawns, she came aboard and set oars into the oarlocks and rowed us through the empty town.

We passed the filling station and saw that the pumps were half-covered in water. They looked like Mrs. McCauley's ancient sisters. Witnessing the doom around them, they stood rigid in silence, their mouths taped over with signs that read "Empty." A board nailed across the station's front door read "Gone Fishing."

A stranded whitetail fawn came out from behind the mailbox at the edge of an oasis we realized was the post office parking lot. The fawn had a hunted look, but it had nowhere to flee to and nervously bowed its head to munch the shrubs planted at the edge of the lot, switching its small tail and staring at us as we floated by.

We rowed until we reached the edge of town and Mrs. McCauley brought us ashore at the brickyard road. She pulled the boat up and tied it to a yield sign then handed me one bucket filled with muddy seedlings. She took two buckets in each of her hands and we headed uphill.

The climb was slow going because the hill was steep and the path rugged and uneven. The buckets were heavy with rainwater and mud and the seedlings were limply hanging over the edges of bucket, so I wondered if all our work was worth the effort. I realized the poor wilting plants were orphans, like me. Yanked out of their homes by life-threatening calamities, they were powerless to resist their captors and completely beholden to us for their welfare. I made a silent pledge to the burpless cucumbers in my pail that they would have the life I had been denied. Those innocent, orphaned cucumbers would be given a home and tender care until all their little baby cucumbers had grown to maturity. I would see to it.

We passed by the brickyard ovens and three stooped men with shovels nodded to Mrs. McCauley as we walked by. They were stoking the brick kiln with heavy shovel loads of coal. Behind them we saw pallets of freshly molded bricks destined for roads and buildings in places much more prosperous than our flooded river town.

Around another bend we came upon a work crew quarrying Decorah shale on the bluff above the brick kiln. The foreman, rigid as a steel shovel handle, stopped what he was doing to aim his hostile eyes at us. Though we were apparently a harmless, stubborn old lady and a young boy carry buckets of mud up the hill, I wondered if we might be shot on sight for trespassing.

Mrs. McCauley told me to keep moving, to keep my eyes on the path ahead, which was studded with fallen shale and broken bricks. An oddly shaped pebble caught my eye, and I glanced back to see if the foreman was still watching us, but he had returned to his quarry men. I picked up the pebble and noted that it resembled a small seashell. I wondered what it was doing on a hillside thousands of miles from the sea. I stuck it into my pocket and hurried to catch up with Mrs. McCauley.

Halfway up, we rested by a waterfall. The skies had cleared, and for the first time in days, I felt the warm summer sun on my skin. Mud had caked my legs, drying in small, tight patches on my shins. We both look as dirty and disheveled as the quarry workers we passed on our way up the hill. I cupped my hand and stuck it under the waterfall. The water tasted like it had been strained through a rusty sieve, but I drank it anyway.

We continued on in silence, not stopping next until we came to the top of the hill. I set down my bucket and panted, taking in the view of the flooded river valley below. We stood at the edge of a small, neatly kept cemetery. With so much rain, the grass glistened like fine emeralds. Polished tombstones of every hue caught the sun and blinded us with luxuriant brightness unexpected in such a somber place.

Mrs. McCauley took me to a bristly burr oak and nearby I saw where Mr. McCauley was buried. "Here," she told me, pointing to the spot near him. "This is where I'll be laid to rest. Since this land is mine, this is where we plant."

She set down her buckets behind Mr. McCauley's grave and motioned for me to do the same. She began to dig out the area right alongside Mr. McCauley's plot. I felt sorry for my burpless cucumbers, but I knew they were better off by Mr. McCauley than in the flooded river bottom below.

I wandered away from her while she worked. I knew Mr. Peter haunted this graveyard as often as he could, trying to work through his share of guilt for the deaths of Mrs. Mary and Brian. I hadn't been allowed to come to their funerals. While Mrs. McCauley was busy trying to bring her plants back from the dead by burying them next to her husband, I had my first chance to visit the graves of my foster mother, Mrs. Mary, and my orphan mate, Brian.

I had no idea where to look for them. There was row after row of tombstones, some so old and decayed their names could no longer be read. Some had even tumbled over and become covered with mosses and lichen. I made my way to the newest part of the graveyard, figuring that would be where I'd most likely come across them. The sky began to cloud over again, and raindrops began to fall once more. I hurried through the rows, but soon all the letters blurred together in my eyes. I came to a small rise above a large open area, and when I looked out over it, I could see hundreds of tombstones.

Thunder sounded from the other side of the river valley, and the skies quickly grew darker. I saw a place that offered some shelter and made my way to it. There, I found myself in a semi-circle of columnar junipers pruned so they spiraled upward. With my back to the junipers, I shivered as the rain poured down, then noticed that before me was a small monument engraved with the names of three people. Two of the names bore both birth and death dates, so at least one person of the trio remained alive. I moved closer, and traced my finger over two names, one of a Sweet Wife and Dear Mother, and one of a Beloved Son.

Suddenly, firm hands on my shoulders shook me violently and then pulled me roughly away. I screamed and kicked and was taken inside a mausoleum and set down. The rigid man from the quarry, the one with violence in his eyes, stared me hard in the face. I was sure he would strike me.

He told me that I must never, ever stand where I had stood. I had no business being there. It was *his* wife and *his* son who were buried in that place—his precious Miranda and his son, Billy. A horrific fire had claimed them both on the same night, a night he would never forget. He wished he'd died instead of them. And now I had trespassed, and not for the first time. He was sure I'd been there before. He'd seen a boy's footsteps near the gravesite. He had half a mind to whip some sense into me. And he would have, he said, if I had been anyone else but Peter's son.

Peter was a good man who had kept the graveyard the peaceful resting place for his poor Miranda and departed Billy. Peter did not deserve such a wicked child as me, a boy who had nearly killed two schoolmates.

Mrs. McCauley came looking for me, and the man explained that I had been babbling nonsense about an orphanage, a Mrs. Mary, an orphan named Brian.

Mrs. McCauley apologized for letting me out of her sight. She had finished planting her garden and was leaving it to Mr. McCauley to get the life back into her half-dead sprouts. Mrs. McCauley promised the foreman she would never let me come near the place again.

Then Mrs. McCauley took me back down the hill, and when we walked past the quarrymen, the foreman was with them, and they all stopped working, eyeing me long and hard to memorize my features. They would not let me get by them again. The men by the kiln were equally keen in their focus. All would see that Albert Park would never again have a moment of peace in their presence.

That night, Mr. Peter put me in my bed and told me I must never speak such nonsense again. There was no such thing as an orphanage nor a Mrs. Mary or Brian who had perished there. He asked me to promise not to trouble other people with my wild imagination.

As I think of that night now— it was so many years ago— I don't remember what I promised. I would not have compromised myself, even then. I know I would have spoken the truth about what I had seen and endured.

I stand now in front of these graves. If I had promised Mr. Peter that night, or any other night, not to speak of my wild imaginings, it would not have mattered or changed anything. I was born not to be believed. I am here because of my parole. I must come here on a daily basis, to work my memory, to try and recall things I'd rather keep forgotten.

I am not, however, required to bring the objects I have kept with me all these years. But I do. I carry them with me in my satchel, and when I visit, I lay them all out in front of these tombstones hoping to elicit some response, some recognition from the spirits that may reside here. I wish they would come and take away these things so I would not be compelled to carry them with me everywhere I go... even into my fractured sleep.

The giraffe, of course, I set down next to Brian's grave. I retrieve from the Zorro lunch box the chapel veil, which I place carefully near Mrs. Mary. The other things—the toy car, the fossil, the agate, the sand-filled balloon, the postmark, the baby food jar filled with ashes, and the paint-by-number Jesus—I look over, but these may belong to others. I don't know anymore.

Do they mean anything to the poor souls buried here? Why is it that objects are so filled with memories yet so unyielding of forgiveness?

Part 2: Living a Lie

Chapter 11—Acts of God

Dear Linda:

I cannot accept your check written for my full hourly rate X my billed hours. I am returning it with this letter and decline your demand to terminate our contract. My action is perfectly legitimate if you recall our countersigned business agreement. I will reference the applicable Force Majeure language and then carefully delineate its implications:

A party is not liable for failure to perform the party's obligations if such failure is as a result of Acts of God (including fire, flood, earthquake, storm, hurricane or other natural disaster), war, invasion, act of foreign enemies, hostilities (regardless of whether war is declared), civil war, rebellion, revolution, insurrection, military or usurped power or confiscation, terrorist activities, nationalization, government sanction, blockage, embargo, labor dispute, strike, lockout or interruption or failure of electricity or telephone service. No party is entitled to terminate this agreement in such circumstances.

If a party asserts Force Majeure as an excuse for failure to perform the party's obligation, then the nonper-

forming party must prove that the party took reasonable steps to minimize delay or damages caused by foreseeable events, that the party substantially fulfilled all non-excused obligations, and that the other party was timely notified of the likelihood or actual occurrence of a Force Majeure occurrence.

Our liaison is still in effect and not, as you put it, "fucking over."

The flowers I sent, the gifts I gave you, our hours and hours of deep conversation are all a component of my service. They have no other meaning than the momentary expression of my fulfillment of a contractual obligation to you. Our weekends of passion are another component. I never said I loved you and indeed I don't. I continue to have the greatest regard for you

Yes, the fact of the matter is that you fell in love with me. This is the Force Majeure clause in full force. It cannot be helped that it happened. I had warned you not to fall in love and gave you plenty of detail in advance about how to avoid it.

I told you of my love affairs to prove to you that women find me irresistible, much to their surprise and heartbreak. I even mentioned the few memorable women, women for whom I still felt a great connection, even though their husbands and boyfriends have threatened me with bodily harm should I ever contact them again. It was for your own good that I went through my romantic history. Yet, it is necessary for a strong bond to be formed between us, particularly when one is in the business that I am in. When one is transforming another's life, a particular bond forms.

But it falls short of love. I did not fall in love with you. It may sound harsh to hear this, but I am not particularly attracted to you. I cannot be blamed for your suffering, and you must continue to carry out the contract you signed with Albert Parque Performance Coaching. d/b/a, Emporium of the Future You. You must remain in my life.

I am not surprised how easy it is for you to throw everything in my face.

Like everyone else I came into contact with during that fateful period of my life six months ago, you were just another potential client of Albert Parque Performance Coaching & Emporium of the Future You, if you will recall, when we met by chance at the Four Inns Restaurant. As the Inn was crowded, we shared a table.

You mentioned that you planned to order your favorite, the pot pie. I pointed out that you might be better nourished by the lentil stew, a dish I respectfully requested the restaurant manager add to the menu, and that I am told is now a favorite there. I introduced myself and handed you my card, and if I recall, you laughed in my face.

"Emporium of the Future You?" You laughed. You see, even from the beginning you did not take me seriously. "What does a boy just out of college know about life coaching?" you said to me.

I held out my business card for your close inspection. I insisted that we share a table so that I could explain myself.

I held out your chair for you and offered to help you remove your coat, but you gave me a haughty look and said you could manage yourself. I was offering politeness, and you took offense. I smiled and thought you rude but said nothing. I took your coat from you anyway and gently pushed you to the table when you sat down.

When I took the flatware and linen napkin from my briefcase, you grew more annoyed, but I explained that one's traditions and etiquette should be boldly asserted whatever the environment even if others around him take offense. It is the signature of the personality, and there is no point in being hesitant. Whatever else others might say about Albert Parque, the fact is that people quickly learn what they must expect from me the moment I enter the room.

I insisted on ordering the lentil stew for you, and you were about to get up from the table and walk away when I quietly told you that I saw you had great potential and that I sensed you were wounded and under-appreciated for your unique qualities. On hearing these words, you hesitated.

I knew then that you would be a client of the Emporium of the Future You.

Women like you—quiet, bookish, with a touch of haughty superiority and who are not particularly striking, but who have a certain memorable quality to their beauty—these are my target market. I could see that your eyes lit up when I labeled you in the manner I did—especially the moment I mentioned what I knew you believed about yourself, that you had decided you were better than other women, women who had settled into their married lives. Women like you are dying to be appreciated, no matter how much you portray yourselves as not wanting attention, of being domestically satisfied. I saw hope glisten in your eyes. I quickly told you then that you were not my type, but that did not mean we could not enjoy a meal together.

You decided to try the lentil stew. Something in the way that you lifted the spoon made me realize that you were much younger than I had thought at first. In your oversized suit, with your hair squashed down and un-styled and your unmade-up face, I had taken you for a harried, middle-aged housewife. I want to be clear that you were not particularly attractive, ever, to me, despite what I had just said to you. I just saw some untapped potential in you, and that was what I had commented on. I never said you were beautiful, but only remarked there was a memorable quality to your beauty.

I write all these things now to clear up the misconceptions that you have had since the day we met. I do not deny there was passion between us. I simply deny what you made of it. I have always been honest with you, and you have told me that you have valued my honesty above everything else. I don't apologize for it now. I have no regrets about the satisfying hours we spent in bed with each other.

Your untapped potential remains, well, untapped. It is for this reason that I return your check and consider our contract void. You may take the time you wish to reconsider our relationship as personal coach and client. I plan on following up with you in two weeks at our regularly scheduled rendezvous location, the Super 8 motel at exit 47. I will be waiting and hoping that you are ready to continue on with our affair.

The Emporium of the Future You awaits.

Sincerely,

Albert Parque

Chapter 12—Identity Crisis

It was Albert Park's death that launched the Emporium of the Future You founded by Albert Parque (at your service). Here I must speak of Albert Park in the past tense, third person, as though he were indeed another person. For to me, he is. And it is necessary for me to conclude Albert Park's story to begin my own.

Though he had never been healthier in his life, Albert Park was soon to die. Albert had just graduated cum laude with degrees in economics and business, had several job offers in hand, a lovely fiancée on his arm, and an impending summer wedding. It was late spring, and the air was humming with opportunity. The lilacs were in blossom and all the bulbs sprouted. All around him, the world propagated, and he had but to settle patiently and await its fruitful conclusions.

I said that Albert Park was a marked man. You wonder why such an apparently harmless and fine young man, on the dawn of adulthood, would draw anyone's contempt or death threats. I can only tell you that the more apparent his prospects grew, the more certain I was that his demise was imminent.

Six hundred guests had been invited to his wedding by his parents-in-law to be, and everyone had returned their expensively embossed RSVP cards to his future parents-in-law's profound satisfaction. They were only too happy to share this joyous occasion with everyone they knew and had rented a beautiful country home with a lovely pond, verdant fields, orchards and rolling meadows. They planned a country dinner hosted by the farm owners, a robust pair who wore matching overalls. An elegant, open-air feast with several courses was planned and his fiancée's parents told everyone they knew, sometimes more than once, that the farmers would be providing hand-churned butter, trout caught in nearby streams, and bread made from hand-milled grains.

His fiancée's parents could not afford such borrowed luxuries, but they didn't care. Their daughter had snagged Albert Park, an ambitious young man who was sure to rise in a Fortune 500 company. Soon she would be well off, and they were sure the wedding was an investment in their own future. They had already planned how they would furnish their in-laws' apartment in the luxurious Manhattan mansion they were certain Albert and his wife would own one day.

Everyone was impressed with Albert Park, none more than his own father. He'd sent him off to a small private Midwestern college not far from the town where he had grown up. It was one of those quaint places that modestly affluent parents can't really afford but quietly accept, paying bloated tuition rates so they can proudly claim the school's name for future use on Christmas cards, embroidered sweatshirts, bumper stickers and rear-window clings. They hope their child graduates, but graduation is not necessarily their end game since even attendance for a few months brings acclaim so long as they carefully use the word "attend" versus "graduate" when speaking of their child's time at the school.

To everyone's shock, upon entering college, Albert became a model student, even though he had not to this point shown any scholarly aptitude. His father was not sure what or who to thank for their son's remarkable turnaround, but quietly breathed many sighs of relief. His son was finally applying himself.

The day I knew Albert Park must die, he had just cleaned out the apartment he'd shared his senior year with his best friend, Peter. Albert had done the lion's share of cleaning and packing, and had had carried most of Peter's things to Peter's car. Even though Peter kept waving him off, Albert didn't quit. He even repacked Peter's things for him, pointing out that Peter's things would travel better because of his packing methods.

Albert Park was that kind of guy—never too busy to help a friend. He'd been an inspiration to the soccer team and was a volunteer coach for the town's high school team. He also helped tutor the high school athletes when the practice and game schedule made them miss class work so they wouldn't fall behind. By the end of the year, he had developed a complex scheduling system that only he knew how to manage, had hired additional tutors to carry the work into the next year, and had left detailed instructions for maintaining the program.

Albert's last words to Peter that day were a reminder for Peter to work on his best man's toast and a happy anticipation of the bachelor party Peter had arranged for Albert a few weeks hence. Then he gave Peter a jocular slap on the back and loudly shouted after him as he drove off a reminder of the best route home, though Albert had not once visited Peter's residence.

I had watched Albert Park for months, and as he gently packed away the mementos from his four years at college, I could see why people thought so much of him. He had everything going for him. Who wouldn't want the future he had coming? Hell, I wanted it, though to be honest, watching him go through his day was like watching a foreign movie without subtitles. He was incredibly affable, even to crabby store clerks whose rudeness left his politeness undeterred. I was mesmerized by the fluidity, the natural interaction he had in his world. How could nothing bother him? I did notice, however, that he was frequently breaking out in hives, and that it was most noticeable when he was having a polite interchange with the rudest of store clerks. In his place, I'm sure I would have decked a few people. But he didn't.

After Albert finished packing his own things, his fiancée came by and took his arm for a final stroll around the campus. They walked in stride with each other, and Albert had his head bent toward his sweetheart. It was a pose he knew she found pleasing. Albert knew well how to please others in those days, and very few thought there was anything amiss under the veneer of his manners. He and his girl were such a handsome pair that everyone envied them.

Albert's fiancée's voice made a pleasant humming sound in his ear, and when she punctuated her sentences with small kisses, he knew that she was satisfied with him, and that was all that mattered. Was he satisfied with her? He knew that he must be. Diana was a luscious, curvy, elementary education major with a fondness for tight, lowcut blouses that accentuated her overflowing bosom. She had sailed through her student teaching assignment and had several job offers at prestigious private schools. She was only waiting for Albert to decide where they would live to make her final selection.

She hid the fact that she did not plan on working after they were married. But the ample supply of job offers was another buxom attribute she liked displaying, so she was cagy about her plans. She found it easy to avoid answering direct questions put to her since neither man nor woman could come away from her unflustered. The gorgeous view of her exposed neckline vaporized any dangling unanswered questions into creamy, sweet scents.

Albert was very fond of Diana's landscape. It was calming to him in the way that a beautiful meadow is calming. Dull, perhaps, if one saw the same thing day after day with no other object than being picturesque. Diana was a small, safe pasture to contain his marital needs. Why should he desire anything else?

Lately, when he had the night to himself, his thoughts busied themselves with two conditions he found perplexing. The first was that he found he did not at all miss his fiancée when she was away. Frankly, it almost felt like a relief, and he was so bothered by his comfort that his hives erupted, requiring vast amounts of ointments to control. He had to ask himself whether he was satisfied with his selection of a fiancée, his major, his career path.

He wrote long letters addressed to a woman long since dead who he had remembered knowing but was not now convinced was real. Still, even a dead, imaginary old lady could suffice as an audience to help him straighten out his confused thoughts.

"Dear Mrs. McCauley," he began each night. "Do I really want this?" When he couldn't come up with a satisfactory reason why he would not, he decided he must be satisfied. So, every night he threw away each unfinished letter, only to find himself starting anew the next night.

"What would be satisfactory?" a different voice was saying to him now. He recognized the voice, but not as his own or his imagined pen pal. Diana's honeyed voice buzzed at his ear, repeating a question about how many swans she should have her parents rent.

"Swans?" he asked. "How many?" Her words made no sense at all to him. He asked her to repeat what she said.

"The farmers have a half dozen, but they think that too many will clutter the pond. Most people went with just two. How many should they go with?" That was what she wanted to know.

For the first time, in years, a dark look flashed across Albert's face, an expression he had not known he still possessed. He turned away from his fiancée to hide it. His fiancée asked again, and I thought Albert would die right there on the spot. He felt the hives blotching his neck, and it was everything he could do to avoid itching. When he didn't speak, his fiancée asked whether something was wrong.

Albert turned to his sweetheart and told her he'd forgotten to retrieve his trophies from the soccer office and there were only moments left until the coach would be leaving for the summer. He apologized for his inattention—he'd become distressed thinking he'd left them behind and forgotten to say goodbye to the coach.

He hurried off, but not before telling his fiancée to procure as many swans as she thought best. He left without kissing her, but she forgave him quickly and called after him with a reminder that they were both expected for dinner at her parents' house later that week.

When Albert arrived at the soccer office, he let himself inside. Knowing no one would be there, he locked the door to be sure he would not be disturbed. He had already collected his trophies, shipped them and bid his old coach farewell. In the darkened office, he sat down and put his face in his hands, not sure whether to weep or to scream.

The talk of the wedding had grown ever more disturbing to him, a fact he admitted to no one, not even himself, nor the Mrs. McCauley. He had dismissed his concerns, thinking it was an ordinary case of bridegroom's nerves. But when the talk of renting swans came up, he understood at last what had caused the heavy feeling that steadily settled on him.

He felt he was being buried alive.

He looked around the cramped, stuffy office and thought about his soccer coach, a man nearing retirement. He switched on the lights and looked at the photographs of all the teams this man had coached through the years. The coach also had an entire wall devoted to photos of soccer players who returned to visit him in later years. Albert had, of course, seen the photos many times before, but for the first time he noticed how vacant the grown men's expressions were in the photos.

He started to see his future self in the portraits of aging, balding, obese businessmen who attempted to cope with the anxiety and stress of business by smoking and drinking too much. When their wives were pictured alongside them, the contrast was often more stark, and the men seemed even more weary, their eye-lids more hung over, their eyes more bloodshot.

Albert hid out there until late that evening when he knew he could get away without being seen. He finally drove off in the middle of night. He knew where he was expected to go, but he set a course taking him in the opposite direction. Of course, I followed, trailing him like a bloodhound, for I knew his scent better than anyone. I was not eager to see him die, and when I met him for breakfast the next morning, I did everything I could to persuade him to return to the life everyone wanted him to live.

Chapter 13—Honest Mistakes

In art, the importance of negative space is a lesson artists learn early. Negative space is everything the subject is not. It is not necessarily background, but can be used in that way to help define the real object of the drawing.

To better illustrate the idea of negative space, think of a silhouette where the subject is depicted entirely in black and the surrounding space is left blank. Here, the negative space provides all of the context. It shapes the subject, without being the subject. The negative space is a bright halo of nothingness that contrasts against the dark void of the artist's imagination.

Many people live their lives in silhouette, not noticing anything around them, and we usually think of these people as normal. I think of them as offensive. Ignorant. Emptier than the void that surrounds them. This, of course, is what Albert Park had been striving for—to fill the outline others had drawn for him with thick, dark life, thereby completing their vision of him. He had no idea how to do create a unique self.

Albert Park was a victim of the enclosing, encroaching negative space that came at him from all sides and confined him in an outline made with permanent ink. His negative space was demanding that he be a businessman, a husband, a provider, with no thought at all to what Albert might or might not want for himself.

The problem for Albert was that he had no idea what he wanted. When he began to think about it, he began to realize what he was *not*, what he had failed to negate, and now, in his sudden flight from his life, what he belatedly needed to disown.

Albert began to destroy the portrait others had drawn of him, erase himself from the picture he was. That morning I saw him dissolving several cubes of sugar into his black coffee, and I did my best to dissuade him from disappearing altogether. He had slept poorly for a few hours in his car and had just found a roadside breakfast place just off the interstate in N_ U_, a small town west of the college he had attended. He had crossed the state border in the wee hours of the morning.

ALBERT PARQUE (Me):	**ALBERT PARK (A.P.):**
a narrator, a young man in his twenties, just six months older than A.P. Nicely, if not expensively dressed, carrying a leather satchel.	a young man in his twenties, is slouched in a diner booth, his collar undone, his shirt mis-buttoned. His hair is uncombed and he has a bedraggled look.
Me: I see you're alone. Do you mind sharing this booth?	A.P.: *Silent*
Me: I'm sorry to have disturbed you.	A.P.: *Silent*
Me: Is this seat taken?	A.P.: *Silent*
Me: *Silent*	A.P.: I'm sorry, mister. I really don't want any company. The place is practically deserted, so you can have your pick of seats. Just not here.
Me: I can see you need a friend.	A.P.: I had plenty of friends. I'm really hoping to just sit here with my coffee.

Me: Look. I can hear what you're saying, but sometimes it's just best to take someone up on their offer of friendship. Give me ten minutes of your time. I'll buy your coffee for you.

Me: *Sliding in opposite A.P.*

Waitress: "Yes, sir? Can I bring you something?"

Me: Fresh coffee for my friend…

Me: …my friend, Albert Park… and an assortment of Danish. Thank you.

Waitress: I'll bring them out right away.

Me: You seem to have a lot on your mind.

Me: Why not?

Me: But you've been that guy they are waiting for, right? What gives you the right to just leave town? You've got responsibilities to be that person they think you are.

A.P.: *Gestures to the opposite seat.* Sure. Don't mind my objections. No one else seems to.

A.P.: You sound down. Miss?

A.P.: Albert Park…

A.P.: My fiancée, my future employers, my future in-laws, my parents…they're all waiting for me back home. I can't face them.

A.P.: …What they want for me. I don't know. They want someone I guess I'm not.

A.P.: I don't owe them anything. I am not responsible for what they have decided they want from me. That person…who I was… seems like miles away from me now. He's a complete stranger to me. I want something new, different, more exciting.

Me: You are the guy who just graduated cum laude? Who chose the degrees you chose?

AP: Yes.

Me: You got down on bended knee and proposed to Diana, didn't you?

A.P.: Yes.

Me: I see absolutely nothing wrong with your life. You've got everything going for you. Job, beautiful girl, a great life ahead. And you want none of it?

A.P.: That's right. And I wish I could give this life away. It's just not me. I did my best but everything, the engagement, the college degrees? They were all wrong. I was mistaken thinking that I'd found my calling. It was an honest mistake.

Me: You've made a lot of promises to people, haven't you?

A.P.: Yes, I have.

Me: Then if you don't plan on keeping any of those commitments you made, there's only one thing you can do.

A.P.: What's that?

Me: You'll have to find someone else to take on that role.

A.P.: What do you mean? Hire someone? To be me?

Me: Why not? Place an ad in a newspaper. I can think of dozens of people who would be glad to be in your shoes. It's easily enough done. I'll help you write the ad, if you want.

A.P.: Well, whoever wants it can have it. It's not really where I thought I'd wind up. I never thought of casting a replacement to take over my life, but it would save me a lot of trouble if someone could just step in and take over

So, I helped Albert Park write up his advertisement. Really, it was just a matter of boiling down the resume Albert had sent out stating we were hiring a permanent replacement for a lifetime position. We placed it in the Help Wanted section. I predicted that he would have plenty of applicants more than willing to give up their rich, unique lives for a chance to be the silhouette Albert thought everyone wanted him to be.

Despite his misgivings about marrying Diana, Albert wanted her to have the best, and he was sure it was not him. He would find someone even better at being Albert Park than he had been, and Diana would have her husband and provider. Albert called to let her know there had been a short delay and her husband-to-be would be at his wedding as planned. She shouldn't worry at all. He had it all well in hand. As always.

Chapter 14—Wanted Man

With graduation money from his father, Albert rented a studio apartment in an old section of town, and we met the next day to plan how he would find the perfect replica to take on his role. Once that job was out of the way, he could start in earnest on his chosen profession. With all the experience he was gaining by finding out who he should be and untapping his true potential, he felt he had a talent for personal coaching. He had so much he wanted to teach others, and he felt the need to lead, push, or just generally give people the swift boot they needed for their own good.

We had discussed the types of men who might make ideal suitors for Diana and found that we had opposing views. I preferred someone who was a capable liar, and Albert wanted a man who would speak only the truth. In fact, Albert had someone in mind, a man who had not actually applied for the job but who we both knew from our days at college.

It was Brian. Brian had been in business classes with us, was a champion debater and clearly was on the road to success. He was also a leader on the soccer team. There had been a split-vote for team captain that year, and since neither Albert nor Brian conceded to the other, the coach for the first time installed co-captains. No one except Albert noticed that there should not have been a voting tie as there were an odd number of voters. Secretly, he thought Brian had rigged the election but knew that calling him out might risk Albert's co-captain status. There was a small chance that the missing vote might have put his own leadership position in jeopardy. A recall didn't sound sportsmanlike either. So, Albert remained on gentlemanly terms with Brian but became, from that point forward, his bitter rival.

Brian for his part hated sharing the spotlight, so he put a lot of effort into making sure he was always placed in a favorable rotation. He bribed the coach by bringing him his favorite pipe tobacco, even though smoking was forbidden in the athletic facility. It was sickening to see how the coach almost treated him like the son he'd never had.

No one but Albert could see that Brian faked being the "team player" whenever it was to his advantage. He sat out bruising matchups, cheering on his doomed teammates and giving inspiring, memorable pep talks that were remembered long after the sting of loss had ebbed. He was sure to be seen on the field after easy wins.

With Brian's quick smile, his handsome, Nordic face and his lack of concern about a receding hairline, he was the favorite on the team who kept the boys stocked in forbidden liquor and friendly nursing students. Whatever they wanted, the pipeline led to his door. His family had long attended the school, so he had sway with the dean, knew his way around administration, and used every connection to his advantage. The team always had the best buses and the best lockers. Everywhere he went on campus, acquaintances stopped him to chat. He was on a first name basis with every department head.

Albert had considered going into business with Brian despite the rivalry. His connections ran deep and would have meant quick success. But Albert couldn't stomach the guy if for only one reason. Brian had naturally caught Diana's eye first, and Albert sometimes wondered whether Brian's interest was the real reason he'd wooed Diana. Albert had always been competitive, but he met his match in Brian. A year or two younger than him, Brian had skipped several grades in middle school, so he had graduated the same year as Albert. Albert was sure Brian had cheated somehow, perhaps had broken into the administrative offices and phonied up the records. If he'd had half the pull in middle school that he had at college, Brian could have easily aced everything.

I reminded Albert that Brian was on the point of proposing to Diana.

"Of course," Albert said. "I know that. He told me himself."

Brian had gone home for Christmas week of their junior year, and both Diana and Albert had stayed at school. "Brian had mentioned that he planned to pick up an engagement ring," Albert told me. "I saw how he looked at Diana. Clearly, the man was on the point of owning her. He had to be stopped." With an uncharacteristically contemptuous expression, Albert explained that Diana had asked him if he wanted to join her for Christmas Eve dinner since Brian was gone and his roommate, Peter, was gone too.

Albert had told me this story many times, but I listened again. It was the story he would have told his future children—how he had met Diana and eventually knew she was the one he would marry. Except neither Albert nor Diana would be marrying after all. So, I was always the only one to listen to the story.

* * *

It was Christmas Eve, and while most of the college town's cafés and restaurants were closed, the take-out Chinese restaurant had a few small tables open, so it was there that Albert met Diana for dinner.

Shortly after hanging up Diana's coat and pushing in her chair, Albert told Diana that he'd just gotten off the phone with Brian. He made a suitably tense face, which made Diana curious.

Diana asked what Brian was up to, then laughingly said he was probably completely bored being at home.

"Brian didn't sound bored," Albert had told her. "In fact, he was just getting ready to go out and meet an old friend." Albert had paused to consider what effect it might have on Diana if he went on. He'd decided to go for it. "Maybe he mentioned her to you?"

Diana had frowned. She spoke the name of a girl and Albert could see the pained look on her face.

"Maybe I shouldn't have said anything," Albert told her. "I guess that might have been the name Brian mentioned, but I can't remember now."

Diana's eyes shot up. "That bastard!" she said more than once. "He's going out with his hometown girlfriend. I *knew* this would happen."

Diana stormed out of the Chinese restaurant and Albert followed her meekly, wishing more people were around to witness that he was in Diana's company. Even in her current state of fury, Diana was bewitchingly sexy. Albert saw his chance for success with Diana, his chance to triumph over Brian. It was now or never.

Albert told Diana how sorry he was that Brian had caused her such grief. He spent the rest of Christmas break consoling her and preparing her for Brian's eventual return. On New Year's Eve, he kissed her, then took her back to his empty room and made passionate love to her, telling her repeatedly how he did not deserve to be with someone so beautiful and how he did not want to take advantage of someone with a broken heart.

Diana said it was probably for the best, especially now that she knew the truth about Brian's history of deceit. She thanked Albert for telling her the whole story about Brian no matter how painful it was for Albert to be honest.

She never spoke to Brian again. From then on, Diana was Albert's girlfriend, then fiancée.

* * *

As we were discussing his replacement, I asked Albert whether he would consider letting Brian have another chance with Diana. The guy clearly was in love with her, and she was pretty taken with him? Why not?

"Brian is so self-involved," Albert said. "The guy can't stop talking for a minute about his grand plans. Don't you find it strange that he's nothing but plans? What he's going to do? What's he done? He's completely selfish. I hate the type. Can we move on? Let's talk about the other option. The other guy is kind and generous. He'd give you his last dollar. He is, as they say, as honest as the day is long. Right?"

"Right."

"Isn't the honest guy a better match for Diana, a safer bet for everyone?"

"No man is an honest man," I told Albert, "no matter what he says about himself. Deep down, *you* aren't."

Albert looked at me, his eyes wide. "You mean because I was acting, playing a role that wasn't really me? That made me dishonest?"

I nodded and could see the light going on in his eyes.

"I see your point," he said.

"This is why she is just much better off with a liar. Someone who admits that he's made a certain number of mistakes. Someone who, when he is at his most convincing, doesn't reveal everything in his hand."

"I'm still not convinced," Albert said. "Diana is the kind of woman who is going to ask her husband every day to be honest. To tell her if she looks nice wearing what she's wearing, or whether she's gotten fat, or whether her hair looks nice. She'll say—be honest, now—she'll look at him with uncertainty, unhappiness in her eyes. Expectation."

"You're right," I said. "But here's the problem for the honest guy. He will be considering her feelings, but also *thinking* the honest truth but not saying it, not right away. That pause is going to immediately create questions in Diana's mind. She'll be convinced instantly that things are terrible, her husband doesn't think she is pretty anymore. Even if the honest man truly loves Diana exactly as she is—not noticing the few extra pounds or the unflattering hairstyle—if he can't immediately affirm her, they will both be doomed."

"So?" He asked.

I told him, "The liar will do a much better job of answering her promptly in a commanding manner, which would give her what she really wants—a convincing illusion that has nothing to do with the truth. No one wants the truth, no matter how desperate they may beg for it."

Albert looked disgusted. He said, "You have a low opinion of the human capacity to be genuine—to want the honest truth. No one wants honesty? Really?"

I pointed out that most people are much better off without honesty. Look at business and politics. The honest people never win. The liars get ahead. Even if they are caught in a lie, and forced to correct themselves, the lie has already resulted in whatever downstream action it was intended to cause. The lie is like a stone thrown into a lake. The stone disappears into the depths, never to be seen again, but the ripples spread. The bigger the lie, the more the ripples. You really can't stop the waves once you've set them in motion. You can't take them back, make it as if none of them existed.

I left Albert to make up his own mind. After all, it was his fiancée he was jilting. I told him that whatever he decided, I would carry out his instructions, but I planned on taking no responsibility for his decision. I had done my best to convince him of what I thought was the proper solution.

Before he disappeared entirely, Albert Park had one last surprise for me. He decided on the honest man after all. That night, he called to arrange a meeting the next day with Diana's new suitor and myself. I'm not sure what finally changed his mind. I think he had ulterior motives. Maybe he hoped the honest man's failings would leave a door open for him and Diana. I don't know. Maybe it was too much for him to learn what I knew—that living a lie wasn't always bad as long as you knew it and used it to your advantage.

Still, maybe Albert had learned from me and had chosen the honest guy hoping he would fail, if only to prove he was superior.

I have to admit that Albert Park could be a very surprising man, and with time I might have grown more comfortable in his conflicted skin. But every time I thought about leading the life he had been grooming himself for with a house in the suburbs, a two-car garage and a job in corporate accounting I couldn't stomach the idea.

The next morning, it was me, Albert Parque, who woke up in Albert Park's small rooms, and went to collect the business cards he had ordered for me. I was very pleased by his selection:

Albert Parque
Proprietor, Chief Executive and Performance Coach
Emporium of the Future You

"Better Yourself for a Better Tomorrow"

Hourly rates. Inquire about our economical weekly rates or convenient lifetime plan.

I touched a few cards in my newly purchased leather card holder and headed off to meet Peter, our former roommate, the honest young man Albert had selected for me to introduce to Diana.

Chapter 15—A Changed Man

Very few people are capable of the courage required to make radical change within themselves. First, change requires a bold ability to ignore the social conventions that most people do not possess. I knew I had the guts to ignore my inner social critic and that it would take sustained belief in myself and my vision to live the way I had been destined to live. I also knew that I must be a social pariah in order to be the man I was intended to be.

A good number of years later, as I walked through my new neighborhood, I looked for the places where I thought other such courageous people might be found. I was eager to greet fellow stalwarts, rugged individuals who might have been good companions, even though such people would not have made for good Emporium of the Future You clients. I was always eager to discuss entrepreneurship, my worldviews, and carry on a spirited debate.

I quickly dismissed every house I came by—there was no one in any of them the least bit bold. These well-kept homes were where people had settled. *Settled.* This word tells you everything you need to know about people's courage. Settled is what people become when they put down roots, thereby shutting off any other options they might have explored. But it also has another meaning, such as when one *settles* one's accounts. A measurement is taken, there is some bargaining, but always a compromise. One reconciles (and I know this from my study of economics) through an imperfect process that is intended to weigh the values of all options but choose only one. Social gravity carries far too much weight, and therefore, I have done my best to avoid settling myself, in both senses of the word.

In my neighborhood, I watched people carrying out the social calculus that they had settled for. They were mowing their lawns in summer, shoveling their sidewalks in winter, attending school, showing up for religious services and spending too much time at work. When I took stock of my life that day, I confronted a man who had come to the end of the period in my life in which I had proven myself more than capable of having the life any of my neighbors had, of settling just as they had done. Everything I had done over the past four years at college had prepared me, like a field crop, for the harvest that society demands.

But at the crucial moment, I had stepped aside and let society's machine trundle past me. Its dust, noise and demands, I had determined, would cut me in my prime. I had better things to do.

I know this treatise sounds exactly like the one people expect from a young, egotistical man. But I was absolutely sure that I understood what motivated most people and I was not at all motivated by the same things. However, I knew most people had not reached their potential. I aimed to show them where they were lacking and what they needed to achieve. This was my vision for them.

So, I made it my business to inspire their dissatisfaction in who they were, and—using my personal tastes as an example—show them what they were missing in life—those higher ideals that only I knew of.

These convictions of mine would, a few years hence, make me a highly sought-after opinionator. I would become much in demand as a business speaker by practicing what I preached—being the perfect disciple of aesthete, I would speak, and others would eagerly listen, paying my fees and hiring me to host seminars. But I would be more than a mere lover of beautiful things. I would provide that translation from making the pursuit of beautiful objects to transforming oneself *into* a beautiful object. I did not consider this hedonism at all. I considered it a pursuit of perfecting *oneself*, which seemed to be an admirable ideal.

I expected to have my detractors. Of course, until recently I had been pursuing the exact kind of life I now abhorred. I was, in a sense, an atheist preaching before a congregation of believers. But as that atheist, I knew the rejected theology better than most people of faith. I knew what drove that faith I was now fleeing. Over a short period, I'd had an awakening of sorts and was ardent in my new path, ready to head in the new direction despite any contradictory evidence. I was ready to be the standard bearer for others.

I was ready to make a living based on my vision. And that day, as I headed to my meeting with Peter, I was completely over the life I'd been preparing myself for, the one that included marrying Diana. I vowed to never return to it.

I already had written a long letter to my fiancée to explain my position and bid her adieu, wishing her no harm. Now I was prepared to reconcile what I owed her by offering her my best friend, Peter, to be her bridegroom.

* * *

Peter and I were scheduled to meet for coffee at a small restaurant near my studio apartment. Peter knew Diana well from their days together in the elementary education program and from her time as my college girlfriend and fiancée. Unlike Diana, Peter did not have an abundant supply of job offers. He was a quiet man and didn't have Diana's obvious and ample physical attributes. While he looked for work as a schoolteacher, he found employment driving a city bus. I thought this honorable though temporary employment for such a man.

As always, I was very gracious to the barista, waving her off when she offered me a paper cup and instead insisting that she fill my thermos for the going rate of a cup of coffee. I explained how my thermos could save her the cost of the cup, washing a ceramic mug, and the cost of later refills. One of the less customer-oriented baristas scowled as he saw me. I knew he complained daily that I took up table space for much of the day but only paid for a single cup of coffee while other customers who might have paid more were forced to stand or left without ordering when the place was crowded. I will point out that such people who leave under these circumstances get what they deserve. They are what I mean by settled people. They have reconciled their lives, and in their accounting of social weight, a well-manicured lawn is more important than a good seat and a fresh shot of espresso at a café.

So, I didn't accept the barista's complaints that I was bad for business. Even when he insisted I pay for a large coffee, I left only enough for the regular size, nodding and smiling as I laid down my change with a reasonable tip. On the contrary, I brought in more customers—my clients. I was more than happy to share my table—the one near the window that was well lit and comfortably situated next to the radiator— even if it meant I had to remove my feet from the opposite chair.

It was there that I was sitting when Peter arrived the morning I planned to explain what I had arranged for his benefit. However, when I told him I had broken off my engagement with Diana, he became incensed—borderline homicidal. I was completely stunned by his unexpected reaction and asked him to explain himself.

He told me I was a complete idiot and wondered what had become of me. Was I going to take no responsibility for commitments I had made to my parents, Diana, even him? I'd sworn up and down that I was passionately in love with her, that there was no one else for me, that she was the one. I had excelled at studies and planned my future. Everyone was counting on me.

Peter, as well, had done everything I'd asked of him in preparing for my wedding.

He did not handle change well.

I explained my business plan to him and gave him one of my new business cards.

He read my cards and looked at me with narrowed eyes. "This is a joke, right?" he said. "You can't be serious. Albert Parque? I've never heard of anything so stupid."

I reiterated my plan.

"You, a tastemaker?" he said. "What gives you the right to decide for others how they should live?" Peter's face grew red. "Besides that, Albert, you can't just drop everything and run. You seemed perfectly willing to go along with the program until now. In fact, you were more than just a mere participant. You insisted on running everything. How do you go from that to just washing your hands of everything. You're responsible to the people you made commitments to."

I explained that, to the contrary, everything in my life prepared me for the step I was taking away from it. I needed a new challenge if I was really going to be the person I was intended to me. I needed to entirely break free.

Peter thought I'd become seriously unglued. He pointed out the strange way in which I referred to the man he had known as if he were a stranger. He suggested I see a doctor. He questioned my mental stability. He pointed out how I frequently spoke of the person I had been as if he were another person entirely.

"Why do you keep talking about yourself in the third person?" he asked. "You say 'Albert did this or that.' Like you are trying to distance yourself from the person you were. It seems sick."

I told him I was perfectly fine. Never better, in fact. The real insanity, as I had recently come to understand it, would be in packing away my intellect and ambition and becoming what everyone around us was becoming—average, middle-class suburbanites who had forgotten themselves.

"I thought we were friends," Peter said. "I thought I knew you." He stormed out the door in disgust.

Not long after, a woman entered and stood nearby searching around for an open table. Since there were none, I offered her the chair that Peter had vacated. I introduced myself and learned that her name was Linda. The same Linda who would become my client, then my lover, then my ex-client and ex-lover. But the double-ex wouldn't for several months, and I truly did my best to leave her in better condition than I found her.

Linda was an obvious mess of contradictory settledness. In other words, she was not quite as average as she could be. She was unaware of her plainness while hoping she was attractive but also unaware that she had possibilities. Her face was round with eyes high on her broad cheekbones. She could have stood to lose a few pounds—not many, just a few. I estimated her age to be around thirty. I suspected she had recently divorced.

I handed her my business card and in her unaware, plain yet attractive manner, she laughed at me.

"Emporium of the Future You?" she said. "Seriously?"

"Of course. I'd be delighted to buy you a coffee and tell you all about the Emporium. Do you take cream?"

She gave me a dismissive look but accepted my offer. "Black. And don't let them add any of that flavor shit. Can't stand it."

So began a series of regular meetings between the two of us at the Four Inns. I immediately prepared an ambitious program for Linda and executed it with missionary zeal. Each morning at eleven-thirty I waited for her to arrive at the Inn from her office, a small accounting firm nearby, then invited myself to her table.

While she clearly had no interest in having a companion, the restaurant was always crowded, and our initial interchange was witnessed by other customers who saw in me a genial, polite young man asking for a chair at the table of an irritable, plain woman. In the early days, customers would turn a hopeful eye to Linda, almost pleading with her to offer the chair to me. Later on, she readily offered up her chair.

At that very first shared meal, I learned quickly about her day-to-day work in the small accounting firm. Instantly, I challenged her. "Accounting is to the soul what cholesterol is to the artery."

"Before you insult the way I make my living, Albert," she said, "why don't you tell me how you actually make a living. You have a job, don't you?"

"Of course. I'm self-employed," I said. "I'm my own boss, employee and manager."

"Of course," she said in a chipper manner. The expression she gave me was brittle and I realized how unhappy she must be. She was only pretending to have enthusiasm and joy for her life.

I placed a lunch order for both of us, insisting she dispense with her usual pot pie and order the lentil stew. She protested, but I quashed her fears and assured her that lentils were better for her. A woman with her type of figure should take better care of herself, I said, with a wink.

This seemed to put an end to her reluctance. I could see that she seemed flattered that someone cared. So, she quieted down and listened as I continued explaining my mission. I was sure that despite her initial resistance—which I took as evidence of her repressed desire to have a different life—she would quickly be a dedicated client.

"Many people go about their everyday lives with a lack of inspiration," I told her. "They work every day like drone bees in a colony, emasculated by societal forces, and return home *defeated* every night. They do all the right things but end up feeling unhappy. Dissatisfied."

"So, you are going to tell me everyone should just run away from their responsibilities like you. Follow their dreams." She watched as I removed objects from my valise.

"Not at all. The opposite, really." I took out the linen napkin, fine porcelain plate with gold trim, and fine silver service I carried with me everywhere.

Linda seemed surprised. Pointing at my place setting, she said, "OK, stop and tell me about this. Why on earth would you carry all that with you? Is it some kind of strange phobia?"

"No phobia. Just an example of what I'm trying to explain. But one moment, please." I stood up and summoned the waitress. I handed her my plate, just as I had done earlier with my thermos. I explained that I wanted my meal served on my plate, genially conveying the deep purpose I felt for this request.

Given the look on the waitress's face, I knew that I had a lifetime of work cut out for me. But since I was a customer in her establishment, she took my plate into the kitchen as I had requested. I returned to my chair, and in a few minutes the waitress brought out my order on my plate and handed Linda a flimsy, disposable plate containing her stew.

"The life you have settled for is that Styrofoam plate holding your stew," I said. "It's the same flimsy plate as everyone else's. Just as there is nothing to distinguish your plate from every other Styrofoam plate in this restaurant, there is nothing to distinguish you from any other person in this restaurant. Is that what you want for your life? Do you want to be drab, boring and disposable like everyone else?"

Linda began eating her stew, and I noticed some spittle dribbling down the corner of her mouth. She spoke through a mouthful of mashed lentils. "Sounds like some new age crap," she mumbled.

"Call it what you like, it doesn't matter. The point is that we have no value for anything. We've designed a world that we consume and dispose of without any thought. We have designed *lives* we consume and dispose of without any thought."

I held out my linen napkin, gesturing at the line of drool down the side of her face. She dabbed but missed it. I could see the woman had no sense of her lack of style.

"Here," I said, taking my napkin back and lifting her chin with my fingertips. I could see that she was observing me closely as I dabbed away, and I wondered if her trust was beginning to grow. One thing was for sure—her skin under my fingertips was soft, her complexion surprisingly flawless. Finally, I met her gaze and saw that her eyes were the oddest shade of green, a feature I hadn't noticed before. I could see myself reflected in her pupils, and although I knew I was a good-looking young man, I could not exactly see in her eyes any acknowledgment of my pleasant features.

To be honest, I didn't ever doubt that she would come around. I really didn't. Unfortunately, in my energetic zeal to make her over, I didn't notice that my elbow was unfortunately close to my plate. When I pulled my hand away from her face, my elbow wound up sunk deep in lentil stew.

Linda laughed lustily, almost spitting her last mouthful of stew at me. "Well, Albert, I need to head back to the office."

I stood up, surprised that the past half hour had gone by so quickly. I pressed my business card into her hand and asked when I might see her again. I was so enthusiastic about the possibility of a role in her life, in enlarging her sphere, that I asked if she had plans for that evening.

"It's soccer night," she said, mentioning an adult coed soccer league she had joined.

"I play soccer," I said. "You do too?" Given her unremarkable physique—she was not overweight, but her physical attributes were not close to Diana's—I was clearly surprised. Frankly, I'd hardly thought of her body at all, even though we were so close together at the tiny table.

"I lettered in high school," she said.

Really? I was co-captain of my college team."

"Why am I not surprised?" she said, a little too archly for my taste.

I knew I could not let that comment go by, so I replied, "I'm more than OK with being led, but when the leadership is slipshod, and I see so many areas for improvement that others are missing, I feel it's my duty to step up. Isn't it good to want things improved, especially in areas where we are investing our energy?"

She had no response to my logical argument. I knew then that I must be a part of her soccer league. I was eager to show her how capable a player and leader I was. I also knew that my professional work with her would eventually take hold and show results. Of course, that would require more time alone with her to implement my full program. I looked forward to playing with her on the soccer field. I'd led others to victory before. I would lead Linda to another type of victory.

"Until later, then," I said, holding the door open for her.

She brushed up against me, gave me a smile, and said, "Sure, Albert. See you later."

I watched as she walked away, noting the firmness of her step—and her hips, which were as perfectly proportioned as the rest of her. She had an athlete's body, a female one. Accustomed as I was to Diana's pliable softness, I found myself straining with eagerness to play against this female competitor and claim a victory either *with* her or *against* her. It almost didn't matter which way it went. Whatever happened, I wanted to emerge a champion in her eyes.

Chapter 16—Another Man

When I arrived at the soccer field, players were gathered in small, still groups. It was a humid summer night, the sky so saturated it felt like an entire cloud had descended onto the field. Sweat already clung to bodies that hadn't yet engaged in sport, and I quickly learned that some of the usual players hadn't turned up that night yet replacements were not actively being recruited. There was a question whether games would be played at all given the heat and humidity.

I wondered whether Linda would be happy to see me at soccer that evening, but I could not let her feelings about me stop what was already destined. I would do everything in my power to change her opinion and make her see the logic and benefits of spending time with me.

On spotting her, I called out and ran to join her. Everyone went silent when I arrived and held out my hand to give her a high five. I was fairly certain that those around her had been talking about me, and I was sure that Linda had told them what she knew about me.

"Albert, you came!" Linda laughed.

Everyone else laughed as well.

"Are you surprised?" I asked, slightly taken aback by the puzzling amount of laughter that heralded my arrival.

"Well, even though I don't know you that well, I guess not. I'm not sure how true you are to your word, but clearly, you are on a mission." The other soccer players laughed again.

Linda introduced me to her friends, and I greeted everyone warmly, sizing them up as potential clients of The Emporium of the Future You.

I noticed how surprisingly fit and trim Linda was in her soccer garb. Her legs were tanned and strong, her arms clearly toned, and her expression so much more robust than it was during our meeting earlier that day. Out of her office-wear, she was a different woman, which showed me how much potential there was to improve her. Already, a change in the environment had elevated her in my eyes. But there was so much more she was capable of. I would be like a jeweler, polishing her and placing her in a setting that matched the luster I imparted.

"I was telling them about your business," Linda said.

A peevish woman with thick, dark eyebrows and short curly hair—whose name I had already forgotten—piped up. "Linda showed us your card," she said. "The Emporium of the Future You." She slapped her thighs and doubled over in laughter. "Really? What qualifies an unemployed, recent college graduate as a performance expert?" She was robust and ruddy from the heat, and I could tell by looking at her she would never attract a permanent partner, not with that blustery attitude and bowling-ball body.

Again, because I had schooled myself to expect resistance, I didn't take her attack personally. "I think we can agree that there are plenty of people with a lot of acronyms they trot out to prove their ability and worth. MBA? CPA?"

"WGAS," the annoying woman blurted out.

"Pardon me?" I had never heard of a business degree with that acronym.

"Who gives a shit?" she said in her annoying voice. Her face grew even redder and sweatier from the exertion of making fun of me. I kept my own temper in check, since everyone I met was a potential client.

I parried. "Exactly my point. I haven't bothered with a meaningless advanced degree. I plan to lead by example."

The woman could barely control her laughter. She was the lowest of the settlers. Clearly, she was in denial over her personal issues as well. I wanted to waste no more time on her.

"Carla, really," Linda said to her friend. "I'm not so sure I'm convinced about Albert's mission, but we should at least try and be civil. He's new around here."

Ah! Already I had Linda's empathy. Good. I didn't want her sympathy, so I gave her a bold and focused look, and could not help licking my lips when I saw her smile with encouragement.

"Carla can be a bit over-competitive," Linda told me. "Helped her to being named on the All-State team four times over. But a bit much," she said with a scolding look.

"All in fun," Carla said, with more of a sneer than a smile. Then her eyes widened. "And speaking of CPAs...." Carla's eyes fixed on a man who came running onto the field.

"Finally," Linda said under her breath.

"Who's that?" I asked as a tall, athletic though somewhat doughy-looking guy approached.

"That's Will, Linda's boyfriend," Carla pointed out with a not too subtle look of glee. "He'll kill you if you even so much as look in Linda's direction," she said.

"Oh, for God's sake, Carla. Stop it for good this time," Linda said.

Boyfriend. My first client had a boyfriend. Rather than feeling my hopes sink, I felt myself rising to the challenge. Good, I thought. Linda can see us side by side. I was determined to win over this accountant boyfriend of hers too. Really, of all the professions one could settle on, a career in accounting had to be the most settled. An accountant? This was what she had settled on already?

"This is Albert," Linda said, introducing me to her boyfriend.

I firmly shook his hand.

"Linda and I had lunch together," I quickly disclosed. I felt it was important to stand up for myself and my rights. He looked like the kind of guy who would require clear boundaries. I'm sure the same would be the case on the soccer field. One needs to follow the rules but play to win. Linda deserved to have male friends, and I had only her best interests at heart.

Linda blushed. "Well, what really happened was that Albert asked to share my table at the Four Inns. You tend to wind up doing that. The place is pretty crowded at lunch."

Will gave me an annoyed look, as if to stake his claim on Linda. "You move pretty quickly, I see."

"To get to know new people and share the companionship of a meal and the camaraderie of a game," I said. "Absolutely." Frankly I found Will overbearing, and the more I knew of him, the more I wondered whether he made a good boyfriend for anyone. Did he intend to cut Linda off from a beneficial relationship with a performance coach? What right did he have? I'd have to speak to Linda about this.

Carla whined, "Are we playing or not?"

"The heat is suffocating," Linda said, lifting her hair off her neck and securing it with a band. I watched trickles of sweat running down the back of her neck. When I looked up, I saw Will's eyes on me.

Will immediately picked up the ball. "Yes," he said, eyeing me. "Our opponents are waiting."

Across the field, a group of overweight, out of shape office workers stood idling. It would not be much of a match, which left Will free to harass his new teammate and attempt to show off for his girlfriend. Every opportunity he had, he passed the ball to Carla instead of to me, and she eagerly took on the goal of defeating me instead of the other team.

Will and Carla huddled whenever they could, obviously plotting how to bring me down. Somehow, they also conspired with the referees so that I was called with numerous unjustified penalties. One time they managed to cut me off, Will's foot connecting with my shin rather than the ball. The hit sent me to the ground, moaning.

"Will!" Linda shouted harshly. "What the hell?" Linda ran to my side to help me off the field then fetched fresh ice water for me and examined my bruised shins.

Will stood nearby saying nothing.

"Really, Will. What's gotten into you?" Linda said. "You've been in a bad mood since the moment you arrived."

She nursed me more, holding ice to my shin, then took a long drink of water herself, wiping her wet face with a towel. She kneeled next to me, pressing ice against my shin. I could see the wet outline of her breasts under her drenched T-shirt.

"I don't think anything's gotten into Will at all," Carla said. "He's just playing to win, that's all. It's Albert who isn't playing by the rules, far as I can tell."

"Oh, is that what you think, Carla." Linda gave her friend a sharp look. "So, what were you and Will doing the entire game, constantly carrying on. I saw what you were doing. You've had it in for Albert since he got here tonight."

She had seen through Will and Carla. Their plans to defeat me were backfiring.

As Carla packed up her things, she said, "Albert looks like a player to me. And I mean *player*. With that ridiculous business of his. The guy's a fraud. I'll see you over at our usual watering hole. Will, are you coming?"

"Are you?" Will asked Linda.

"Are we inviting Albert?" Linda said.

Carla took one look at Will and then answered her friend. "*We* are not."

Looking directly at me, Linda replied to her friends, "Well, then, I guess *we* won't be coming."

"Then you'll have to find your own ride home," Carla said. "We're outta here."

Will and Carla left without another word. I saw them look back at Linda and me just before they were out of sight.

"I'm really sorry about how you were treated tonight," Linda told me.

"You have nothing to apologize about," I said. "You can't control how other people act."

"No," she said, sitting next to me. "I can't. But I played along."

I gave her a puzzled look.

"Before you got here," she said.

"Oh?"

"I did make fun of you," she admitted. "Actually, of your business."

"Oh." I could see she was starting to come around, at least with an apology. Maybe that would open her mind to other possibilities. I said nothing and let her continue.

"I'm sorry," she continued. "I'm sure when I understand it better, it will… will make more sense." She sounded sincere. "But honestly, Albert, it does seem kind of preposterous. You are, after all, just out of college. The whole thing seems a little over the top, don't you think?"

"No, not at all. In fact, if you'd like, we could discuss it more over a drink. I mean, since your plans have changed." I smiled, then winced when I stood up and put pressure on my leg.

"Well, you're right about that," she said. "And I better stay with you longer… since you're injured and all. And possibly dehydrated."

"Yes, that's true," I said.

"I need to sit with you longer while you rehydrate," she said, obviously having convinced herself of the necessity of spending more time with me. She carried our gear off the field, and we decided that she would drive my car someplace for a drink. Since she had ridden to the game with Carla, there really was no other option. She was at my mercy for transportation, and I was at hers. Perfect. I would have the next several hours to let her fuss over me, and I had no time to waste in making my case.

Chapter 17—In Denial

I took Linda to a quiet sidewalk café a few blocks from my home. It was one I hadn't visited yet. I had heard it was rather exclusive, and in truth the service was reliably stuffy, sometimes to the point of condescension. This snobbish attitude was not necessarily a bad thing. It could be the sign of the restaurant's high quality or perhaps a desire to attract the type of clientele that would have to earn the staff's respect.

I saw this attitude as a challenge. I was determined to be seen as a guest deserving of attentiveness, and I knew that to do this required that I match their high expectations with equally demanding requirements.

While we waited outside for what I determined was the best table—a small, intimate spot near the window—we watched a storm brewing. Lightning raced from cloud to cloud, and within clouds, but not so much as a drop of rain fell, nor did any lightning hit the ground. However disagreeable the sky, it kept to itself, brooding and worrying with muffled thunder. The steamy atmosphere threatened but remained unyielding of its stormy potential.

Linda and I were initially seated at the last open table on the patio, one closer to the dumpsters than anyone should be and far away from the wait stand. I was undeterred, of course. I told Linda that our placement was only temporary, and instructed our waiter to let us know the instant the perfect spot opened up.

The waiter walked away nodding, but I knew I would have to keep my eye on him and made a mental note to learn the manager's name so I could seek him out if necessary.

Linda did not seem to be put off by the location of our table. "Albert, it's a good ways away from the trash. We're not right next to the kitchen. It's quiet. I'm not sure what you're complaining about."

She proved again that she had much to learn. She cut me off when I attempted to order for her. "Just give me a beer," she said to the waiter. "Whatever you have on tap is fine."

I ordered a brandy, though I knew my funds were dwindling. I believed, however, that it was just a matter of time before I had a solid list of clients lined up and billable hours being billed.

Almost immediately after our drinks came, the waiter departed and I had to summon him again. When he arrived, I pointed to the candle on our table, which had practically run out of wax, and asked for one that was newer. He mumbled and walked away but returned shortly with a newer one, lighting it and setting it in front of me.

"I hope you find that satisfactory," he said with a barely hidden scowl.

I thanked him with an authoritative tone, making sure to look directly in his eyes. Training waiters to be respectful took time and constant effort. But I had to set a certain standard for those around me and more often than not show them the proper way to behave.

Linda gazed at the sky and our surroundings, content and satisfied. "I love this kind of evening," Linda said. "The atmosphere is so electric you can feel it. It's completely overflowing with pent-up energy. It's like…" she took a sip of her beer, then said, "it's like the best part of anticipation. Something is coming, but it's not here. All the possibilities are out there, like Christmas, let's say. All the packages are wrapped up under the tree. You don't know what's inside, and the excitement of waiting is such a thrill, even though you wished you could tear into those boxes."

I nodded.

"You know how it is when you get past a *certain age*," Linda said. "You learn, after time, that no matter how much you wanted that toy you couldn't live without, once the boxes were opened and that thing was in your hands… well, there's nothing left to look forward to at that point. The fun is really over. Once I got to be eleven, or twelve, Christmas left me exhausted and depressed. It got to the point that I really started to dread the letdown. Isn't that stupid?"

"No," I said. "No, it's not." I could see, as she finished her wistful speech, how much there was in her that could be perfected. And even more, her yearning told me how much she needed me. Life had disappointed her. Clearly, she needed to close that gap between how she was and who she could be. I knew that I needed to impress upon her the urgency of this work, and the way to do this was to make her hate the wideness of that gap.

"That's what I'm trying to tell you," I said. "That's really what my business is all about. Turning the excitement you no longer feel about your life into an actionable result. It's a fine balance between striving and arriving."

"Thing is," she said. "In real life, you learn the truth about things—like those toys you thought you couldn't live without. You learn that, indeed, you can live without them. And once you learn that, there's really nothing left. You settle into whatever rut you find yourself in. And that's that."

Linda was in a perfect place to be coached. "See? That's my point. Why settle?"

She nodded. "I do see. You grow up and get a job. End of story." She leaned back in her chair.

The waiter came by and collected our empty glasses, leaving behind refilled ones.

"Look, Linda." I said. "You and I are both whole, resourceful, capable and creative. When I talk about the Emporium of the Future You, that's exactly it. It's a conversation, like this one. I accept what you are saying right now about how people settle. You sound, without saying it, that you are unhappy that you have settled."

She watched me, her cold glass sweating, her eyes wet.

"What would make you happy?" I said.

She smiled a little too brightly. "Lots of money to buy whatever I want."

I laughed and pointed out, "That sounded sarcastic."

"I know. But no matter what I just said, I am still that kid waiting for Christmas. Thinking that just the right thing is there, under that tree. The problem is that I need to change my attitude to see things differently. To accept my lot."

I said, "Yes, money can allow you to buy things that make you happy. Is that what you want?"

"Oh, Albert. I don't know." She had a distant look in her eyes. "You know, you are the first person who ever asked me that question? What would make me happy?"

I suspected as much. Certainly, that no-good boyfriend of hers had just his own interests in mind.

At last, the moment had arrived for me to present my business pitch. "Would you like to have a way of figuring out what would make you happy, and how to get there?"

"Isn't that the line you tell all the girls? You are just the guy to make them happy? To give them what they want?" She took a long drink then ordered another. "It's the oldest con in the book."

"It's not a pickup line. Linda." I cast out my professional line. "Coaching is strictly peer to peer, expert to expert." Then I blurred it. "Beyond that, relationships sometimes deepen as we explore the possibilities."

I saw her expression sour. "So, not strictly business, right?" She licked her lips, unaware of the signals she was giving off. She was not the only one in denial.

I glanced in the direction of our waiter, noticing that the good table had opened up. He saw me and looked away. Almost instantly, another couple was seated there. He glanced at me once again, smiling.

I had bigger fish to fry. I turned back to Linda and said, "We're adults. Things happen between adults. Why shut yourself off to the possibilities?"

I knew then I'd have to disclose a few matters. Relationships, even business ones, required honesty. Trust. I needed to gain her confidence, so I said, "The most important part of every relationship is honesty. Complete honesty. No holds barred. Don't you agree?"

She nodded. "Of course. You have to be able to trust the other person."

"No one gets what they want out of any relationship, business or not, if barriers remain. My job is to remove the barriers you've put in the way of getting where you need to be. And to do that, you need to be completely open and honest with me, and I with you. You need to trust me. You may not like what you find out about yourself. You may not like what you find out about me. That's how it works."

She considered this. "Still, with all this emotional honesty transpiring between us, I can see a lot more going wrong than right."

I took a leap. "So isn't that what life is about? Making mistakes? Learning from them?"

She considered this too. "I suppose. But I still feel like I'm being conned."

"I have nothing but the most honest, deeply felt conviction in you. I have that in all my clients or I wouldn't be with them. The only way to turn things around is to work together. Very closely." A few drops of rain began to fall.

The waiter came by and dropped off our tab, and I could see that the restaurant staff was clearing out the rest of the customers and cleaning up for the night.

"I didn't realize how late it was," Linda said. "And, I forgot that you're the one with the car. Let me pay the tab, since you provided transportation."

I did not accept her logic in paying, but allowed her to cover my brandies. "A down payment on my fee," I said.

"Fee," she said. "Right."

I opened the car door for her, and she brushed against me as she got inside. The rain really began to come down as we drove through the city. At her apartment, we sat in the car waiting for the rain to let up so she would not be drenched. I held out one of my consulting agreements, suggesting that we could discuss her questions later.

She snapped on the dome light and immediately began to read it. "Acts of God," she said. "Kind of strange to be reading this given the weather. It looks like a deluge out there. Is that a sign?"

"Oh," I said, "the Force Majeure language. It's just a standard contract clause."

She began to read it softly, as if it were a bedtime story. "A party is not liable for failure to perform the party's obligations if such failure is as a result of Acts of God (including fire, flood, earthquake, storm, hurricane or other natural disaster), war, invasion, act of foreign enemies, hostilities (regardless of whether war is declared), civil war, rebellion, revolution, insurrection, military or usurped power or confiscation, terrorist activities, nationalization, government sanction, blockage, embargo, labor dispute, strike, lockout or interruption or failure of electricity or telephone service. No party is entitled to terminate this agreement in such circumstances.

"If a party asserts Force Majeure as an excuse for failure to perform the party's obligation, then the nonperforming party must prove that the party took reasonable steps to minimize delay or damages caused by foreseeable events, that the party substantially fulfilled all non-excused obligations, and that the other party was timely notified of the likelihood or actual occurrence of a Force Majeure occurrence."

She looked over at me and said, "I'm always prepared, I can assure you. For most of those circumstances."

A loud clap of thunder shook the car.

She asked, "So, you have an umbrella then? That you'll lend me?" She had an inviting tone in her voice. "You know—to prove that you would take a 'reasonable step' to minimize the damage here? Like to my hair?"

I smiled and leaned close to her, reach into the back seat for my umbrella. Suddenly, a loud banging came from outside the driver's door. Will was hitting my door hard with his bare fist.

"What are you doing with my girlfriend?" He demanded.

I took the umbrella and stepped out.

"I repeat," Will yelled. "What are you doing with my girlfriend?"

"I heard what you said."

The poor guy was soaking wet, but I'm sure if I had offered him space under my umbrella, he wouldn't have budged. I certainly didn't need him any closer to me with his idiotic threats. I had nothing to explain.

He stood and threatened, but I didn't move. I just calmly said, "I don't need to explain anything to you. Go home, Will."

"What do you mean you don't need to explain anything?"

I heard Linda opening her door.

"Linda, stay where you are," I said.

Growing even more furious, Will said, "You started moving in on her the second you arrived tonight."

"Is that what you think?"

"That's what I know." Will peered into the car. "Get out of the car, Linda!"

"She'll do no such thing," I said. "She's an adult. She can decide for herself what she wants to do."

"Oh, she can, can she?" Will shouted.

I couldn't let Will threaten Linda's growing confidence in me.

Will persisted. "Linda, don't be fooled by this guy. He's a fraud. Carla told me all about this phony business of his. It's a joke." He moved closer to the passenger side of the car.

I heard him start to open Linda's door, but she didn't budge. Instead, she said, "Go home, Will."

"What?" Will was now inflamed with jealousy and indignation. "You have to be kidding me. He's already suckered you?" He took a few steps back. "You're telling me to go? You want him him to stay?"

She repeated herself. "Will—just go home."

Disbelief came over his face. "Wow. I would never have thought you'd let this kind of a guy get to you. Just—wow."

He stalked around the car and came to face me one last time. "Unbelievable," he said, then shook his head. "Unbelievable. A slick talker like you, in no time flat, and she's fallen under your spell."

He finally walked away, but not before one last warning. I was not surprised by it. In fact, I expected it. I welcomed it. It was the last barrier that Linda would need to face and I would help her around it.

Will said, "Remember. I warned you, Linda. I see these kinds of guys all the time, and he's the worst kind there is. I can't believe how easy it's been to make a fool out of you."

It was not the last time I would hear someone tell a client how I'd make her a fool. Yes, you heard that right. I only accepted women as clients. I had no interest in another man's potential, no interest in perfecting someone who might simply become more of a challenge to me. I had no need to hear a man praise my work with him. In fact, I knew no man would believe that I could have anything to do with his improvement. Men could be counted on to discredit other men's roles in their lives. How many sons thought appreciatively of their fathers? How many younger brothers fought their elder brothers, rather than accept their guidance and wisdom?

Chapter 18—A Life of Quiet

Desperation

It wasn't long before Linda dumped Will. She and I began to meet regularly for lunch and had long conversations that extended past a normal lunch hour. This led to dinners. She eventually invited me to dine at her home. As I insisted on keeping my domicile as a place of business, I did not reciprocate. But I did accept her offer.

I knew how necessary it was for a client to open up and be vulnerable so that essential breakthroughs could occur. Allowing me into their most sacred spaces, their private residences, the inner sanctums of their homes—where both possessions and fetishes were unguarded, essentially naked to the eye—was the fastest way to evaluate how settled a client was. The random knick-knacks and cheaply made personal appliances, like the horror of a cheap toaster, said much more about the state of the owner's mind then their résumés.

Linda was no exception. Tacky horror novels lined her wicker bookshelves. Thrift-store furniture and other hand me downs—all of them repaired and cleaned— were mixed in with extremely modern, brand new pieces. Some might have considered her decorating "adventurous," even "cutting-edge," but I thought it was a sign of disorder and uncertainty. Therefore, I immediately offered Linda recommendations. I suggested that she strip down to almost nothing in terms of decor. Stirring up this private place of hers could result in the essential chaos necessary for her to break free.

She seemed disappointed that her home was not to my liking.

"I don't mean to insult you," I said gently. "It's just that… well, there's so much here. It's like perfume that's too heavy. You miss the essence of the person."

"I guess I see your point. It might be overwhelming."

"That's one word for it."

"On the other hand, lots of people have thought it charming. In fact, I've been asked more than once to help friends decorate."

This prompted more of a speech than I initially thought of making. "People mistake abundance and profusion for expertise," I told her. "People think that because owning lots of expensive cars makes you knowledgeable about cars. Not at all—it just means that you know how to surround yourself with expensive toys. No one knows how that rule of abundance and profusion operates better than me. People wrongly think my lack of life experience makes me less than an expert in teaching life skills. The truth is that it's my purity from too much influence—from too much living—that makes me influential about the topic. I'm very selective in how I live my life. I'm not going to approximate living it by immersing myself in what people commonly consider life routines like an office job, a wife, a two-car garage."

I went on to tell her that Betrand Russell had said much the same thing. "It is preoccupation with possessions more than anything else that prevents us from living freely and nobly."

If Linda didn't my opinion was valid, I thought she might find Russell's compelling. But who knew what a woman who liked horror novels thought—or knew—of British philosopher-mathematicians. I could see by her confused look, though, that she understood she might be living a lie, so I asked her the obvious question.

"What's your own opinion of your decorating? Do you really like being surrounded by all of this stuff? Is it essential or superfluous in your life? 'Our life is frittered away by detail… Simplify, simplify.'"

"Is that another Bertrand Russell quote?"

"No, but from someone else just as wise—Henry David Thoreau. And speaking of Thoreau, he said 'Age is no better, hardly so well, qualified for an instructor as youth, for it has profited so much as it has lost.'"

She smiled at that one and began to look in earnest around her house realizing that I was right. I offered to help her eliminate the excess from her life. In the days that followed, I led the purging of her household, taking many carloads of things to consignment stores and charitable institutions. Indeed, I asked her whether she wanted to be listed as the contact for the consignments or have the receipts for the donations. She did not. She said I should keep whatever payment I could get from these things and us it as payment for 'services rendered.' She insisted she wanted nothing more to do with her old things.

In no time, her house was nearly clutter-free. Except for a large armoire, a table, a few chairs, a mattress, and some necessary personal items, she was unencumbered. I gave her the only book she needed and took away all of her horror novels. I knew Henry David Thoreau would offer her good company and helpful advice as she navigated through her much-improved environment. I pointed out a key phrase here or there while we both sat on her floor:

"Most of the luxuries," I told her, "and many of the so-called comforts of life, are not only dispensable, but they are hindrances to the elevation of humankind."

Because I was well acquainted with Thoreau's philosophy and knew my role vis-à-vis possessions, I did not consider it ironic or wrong to keep a few of the items Linda had decided to jettison. So, when I went home at night, I had a comfortable sofa, elegant—but not terribly so— and a wonderful desk where I could conduct business. We had both profited by our business relationship.

Needless to say, Linda had abandoned Will with about as much thought as she applied in getting rid of the huge armoire, which housed her rare pottery. "A positive hindrance to my elevation," she remarked, both of Will and the oversized armoire. Naturally, I helped remove the many pottery items she had amassed.

I asked if she knew where I could bring the collection, as someone else who liked being hindered might offer a good price for them. She knew of a collector, and once my car was completely loaded with pottery, I drove off. When I first learned how much people were willing to pay for old pottery, I was stunned. Since Linda no longer wanted anything to do with her past, I knew it was best for her not to know how much her collection was worth. She was making so much progress, I knew she wouldn't want anything to slow her down. So, I kept the money from selling the collection and it easily covered my expenses for several months.

Unexpectedly, I had stumbled into a profitable side venture. What was true for Linda was true for all my clients. Once they decided to accept my challenge and unburden themselves, I profitably disposed of their unwanted baggage.

In no time, I became a master haggler. I was always unfailingly courteous and expected the same in return. I did my research, so I knew the value of the things I was selling, and I knew what a reasonable mark-up was. I learned how to get top dollar, how to display my client's wares most favorably, where the blemishes were that needed hiding. I learned when to walk away. I learned the value of saying no and of saying nothing at all.

I also learned how to keep my clients from becoming unnecessary parties to my side venture, reasoning that their progress could often put them in a fragile, excitable state of mind. One woman, who eventually had to be legally restrained from contacting me, unfortunately experienced a setback and nearly attacked me when she learned an heirloom piece of jewelry had been sold as part of my "unhindering" process. She flew into a rage when I reminded her of the contract between us. I had to replay the audio recording I'd made during one of our coaching sessions in which she clearly stated that she wanted to break free from the past.

This woman said she hadn't meant that she had granted me permission to sell jewelry that had been in her family for a century.

I explained that I had done nothing of the sort. At that time—and I kept this from my clients as a trade secret—I never got involved directly in the unhindering. A variety of associates managed all those delicate transactions, handling them independently while I personally coached the client in another location. I'm sure a few months later she didn't even miss the jewelry.

The situation with this particular client illustrates why my network of skilled partners became so important to me. It was because of this network of carefully arranged, discreet partnerships that I was able to finance my business, thereby offering my personal coaching free of charge. It was the perfect arrangement. All of these relationships, from my trusted pawn shop, to the coffee shop where I found new clients, to expensive restaurants where I dined with existing clients, to the barbers and tailors who kept me looking my best—all of these contributed to the success of the Emporium of the Future You.

I'm sure to some it might seem like selling my client's furniture, clothing, cars and jewels appeared at worst to make me a criminal and the money I received to be ill-gotten gains. But I didn't think of it that way.

How clients valued their things didn't enter into the equation. I was on a mission to help them appreciate the value of their non-material lives. If someone wanted to pay high prices for things that my clients no longer wanted, that was not relevant to the real value I was adding to my clients' lives.

Working with Linda helped me discover my niche, the types of women who would most benefit from my services. I knew that my mission was not only to improve my clients, but myself as well. I was on my way to being the best man I could be.

Chapter 19—Businessman

About six months into my new business, I had a regular base of clients and steady revenues from the sales of their unwanted material possessions. I began to search for larger quarters and a separate space to use in conducting my business.

I had heard that many rental properties were available at low prices in a depressed area of the city away from where I lived. The low prices and different location seemed opportune, offering the possibility of expansion into an untapped market. I circled a few "for rent" ads and closed my office for the day to investigate.

Winter had just arrived, and the forecasters warned of icy conditions in the days ahead. Given the forecast, I thought it best to leave at home my car, which had been given to me by a grateful client. I boarded a bus to head across town. My route required a transfer and the driver of the second bus was none other than my friend Peter.

He smiled and nodded, we shook hands, and I found a seat directly behind him.

Peter and I eyed each other in the rear-view mirror before he said, "Nice coat." He was referring to the expensively tailored wool coat I wore. "Looks warm."

"It's vicuña wool," I said. "It comes from a South American camel-like animal that produces only about a pound of wool a year." The vicuña was believed to be the reincarnation of a beautiful Incan maiden who had received a coat of pure gold after consenting to the advances of an old, ugly king. The legend held that you could be killed for wearing such a coat if you were not Inca royalty.

"How much did that set you back?" Peter asked.

"I don't really know. One of my clients gave it to me."

I had heard from my haberdasher that vicuña yarn can cost up to $3,000 per yard, meaning a man's coat can cost nearly $20,000 dollars. When I learned this, I thought it best to keep the coat. It fit me perfectly. But I didn't mention the cost to Peter. He was, after all, a bus driver. He certainly could have done better for himself, but obviously had chosen not to. Hearing the value of my coat would do nothing to change his mind or his world.

"Clients? Really?" Peter said, and then pulled his bus to the curb to pick up a few more passengers.

An icy wind blew through the doors. I was very glad for my vicuña.

"Yes," I replied. "I have several now."

"A while back you told me about your performance coaching business. That the one?" Peter asked.

"Yes."

Peter peered at me again in the rearview mirror. "The Emporium of the Future You?"

He had remembered.

"Yes," I said.

"And you get paid in coats?" Peter sounded shocked. Or irritated.

"Sometimes," I said. "But that's not really the point."

"Well, you seem to be doing well, judging by how you dress. Do your clients take all of your suggestions well?"

"It's a long process."

"And apparently very profitable."

"People don't change overnight," I said.

"You seem to have changed," Peter said.

He pulled his bus to the curb again and discharged a few passengers. We had arrived at that part of town where the rental properties were available. The passengers who exited had weary looks on their faces as they trudged off. Every building in this area was dilapidated. Many were empty and available. Some appeared condemned and had boarded up windows and padlocked doors.

"What brings you to this side of town?" Peter asked. "Clients? The area could use some improvements, but it doesn't look like it's the kind of improvement you're interested in." He gave me another look in the mirror. "In fact, it looks like the business opportunities over here are pretty limited for your type of work. You won't see many folks on these streets wearing fancy wool coats."

I saw my stop ahead and stood up, saying, "I'm looking into some business property, and despite your negative attitude, I believe I could make a difference here."

Peter pulled up to the next intersection and stopped. "—Maybe as a slum lord," he said with a sneer.

I chose to ignore his remarks. He had dismissed me and was not interested in anything I had to say.

As I prepared to step off the bus, Peter said, "Oh, by the way. You'll be glad to know that Diana has recovered from what you did to her. She's going to be married tomorrow. Not that you care." He opened the bus door.

"Of course I care. You know that I wanted her to find someone suitable."

"Well, suitable or not, she's getting married, tomorrow."

I had to know, so I asked, "Who is she marrying?"

"Oh—you didn't get an invitation? I'm shocked." Now that he could look me full in the face, and I could see his, I recognized the full force of his opinion of me. "This is my last stop so you have to get off here."

I stepped off the bus, then turned and said, "I'm surprised at how angry you are. I always had nothing but the best intentions toward Diana."

"Intentions. Right," Peter said. "You destroyed her relationship with Brian, then when you were tired of her, you dumped her, justifying your use of her. Now you're passing yourself off as some kind of savior to other people. I can't believe that anyone could be so easily duped."

It was pointless to try and convince Peter of the importance of my mission.

Peter glared at me through the open door, then said, "Fortunately for Diana, Brian forgave her. He took her back. That's who she's marrying. Have a nice day. The return bus comes in an hour. My shift is over as soon as you get off the bus."

Peter drove away. A freezing rain was coming down and I looked for a place to take cover until it rain let up. There were no coffee shops or restaurants in this part of town. The only open business was a street corner bar. I ducked inside, and even though it was not even noon, I ordered a stiff drink to warm myself, not trusting that the bar coffee was up to my usual standards.

I could hardly believe the news that Diana was being married the next day to Brian, the last person on earth I thought she should marry. She deserved so much better. I had let her down by not making certain she had selected a better mate.

After a second drink, I knew that my plans for the day had to change. I got onto the next bus that came by, returned to my apartment and packed for a pre-wedding visit to Diana. The conditions were treacherous, but I knew that I had to take a chance.

Diana deserved the best that the Emporium of the Future You had to offer, so I set off in my car to her home a few hours away. If she was lucky, I would arrive in time to set her straight.

Chapter 20—Best Man

Many years have passed since that day I drove frantically to rescue Diana from her doomed wedding. That same day, Albert Parque died. Every time I come to this particular hill and stand in front of the graveyard entrance, the events of that day go through my head.

I'm not fond of cemeteries, particularly this one, but I come here because I am legally required. It's a condition of my parole. I won't go into the circumstances of the charges to which Albert Park was found guilty. My only comfort is that it was Albert Park who was found guilty. I share nothing with that other man except his name, which I have gone by since shortly after my birth. But that is a circumstance of my life, not a fact. Unfortunately, this mistaken identity has ruled my life

To be honest, like every person, my memories grow hazier as the years go by. So why does any of it matter—the quarrels, the crimes, the heartbreak—when an entire life gets summed up in deeply engraved letters and dates on a tombstone? The rest is forgotten. Humans are, in fact, forgettable. I cite this evidence—time itself considers nothing at all of our biological remains and allows the earth to reabsorb us and repeat our errors with another generation of fallible, inept, incomplete specimens. Nothing changes, and we go on telling and retelling our history, making our excuses and blaming others for our errors.

I am legally required to tell you what the inscriptions read on tombstone 26-A, and that is the only reason I stand before it now.

While I object to my punishment—which seems arbitrary and ridiculous—I am in fact a law-abiding citizen—and even a simpleton can easily conclude that I am given the number of lawsuits I have filed, the majority of which have been dismissed. I sue to make the point that I believe in the law, much like the faithful regularly attend mass to prove they believe in God.

Thus, while I continue to protest my sentence, I carry it out and accept that I must continue to do so because my appeals have been exhausted. Even the high court no longer accepts any new casework submitted by Albert Park, Esquire.

I stand near a semi-circle of columnar junipers pruned so they spiral in whirling corkscrews. Before me there is a small monument (numbered 26-A) engraved with the names of three persons, only one of whom remains alive. I am legally bound to tell you who lies buried here.

They are:

Mary, Sweet Wife and Dear Mother

Brian, Beloved Son

* * *

My car antenna shivered, whipped by the wind and rigid from the freezing rain. I was sure that it would be snapped off entirely as the thick coating of ice made it lose all of its normal flexibility. Given the miserable driving conditions on that day so many years ago, I initially thought it best to keep my radio on if only to hear about road hazards and possible alternate routes.

A radio voice announced, "No travel is advised throughout the area due to dangerous road conditions. Meteorologists report that conditions like those today have not been seen in the past several decades. The barometer is plunging to all-time lows, and later today the freezing rain will switch to full blizzard conditions. A foot or two of snow is not out of the question. Authorities state that stranded drivers may not receive assistance quickly due to the high volume of accidents reported. Even emergency vehicles are finding the roads impassable..."

I tried to tune into another station, maybe one playing opera, but the same dire warnings were on every station. I shut the radio off. Nothing would dissuade me from my plan, though the driving conditions were the worst I had ever experienced.

I drove with my car window partially open, as that was the only way to ensure I could see something and not have to stop my car to scrape the ice from my windshield. I drove as fast as I dared, passing numerous unfortunate motorists whose cars had slid off the roadway into the ditch.

I knew the way to Diana's house by heart because she had grown up in the town I and my father had moved to in my early teens. The years before I lived there seemed even further away now, and I forget them, replacing them with the wonderful memories of growing up near Diana. I knew what I felt for her. As I drove home to prevent her marriage, I was certain I hadn't made the mistake my clients always made—to fall for the illusion, the romantic nostalgia for things that never were.

I'd seen this failing often with my clients. They pined at times for the present I was trying to rescue them from. This is why my work was so arduous and so obviously necessary. I needed to make them understand that the reality they thought they had lost was nothing but an illusion to begin with. They had been conditioned from birth to want the very things—corporate jobs, comfortable middle-class possessions, bowling friends, affectionate spouses—that had been their downfall into the less-than-ideal world of settling. I found myself constantly setting them straight, guiding them to accept nothing short of the ideal. And until they were clearly on the right path, all of the trappings they had surrounded themselves with were distractions, petty ones to say the least.

Sometimes it was hard for them to shed the material items and ineffectual relationships in their lives. I could see their quandary, but never empathized. I had to maintain my distant superiority and show them what they could achieve. But some would never succeed, and I knew those hopeless cases would ultimately have to be dropped from my client list.

There were others who cut their association with me prematurely no matter what I did to convince them they were wrong. Linda ultimately became one of these cases. So much potential—and so much of my valuable time—was lost on her.

So be it. If a client jettisoned her association with Albert Parque, I couldn't help it. And I lost no sleep over these cases. I knew I was in the right.

I was convinced of that even more now. The closer I got to Diana's hometown, the more persuaded I became that I had to stop her wedding. She was an ideal, maybe my ideal. Only time would tell. I certainly couldn't let her believe the illusion of Brian was her ideal. I grew sick thinking about it, and angry with my former friend. How could Brian deceive her and lead her to an uninspired lifetime in the suburbs.

So, I drove without stopping. My head had never been clearer, my vision never more focused. My hands gripped the wheel, and I drove on without fear. Ahead, traffic suddenly slowed, and we wound around a postal service semi that had jackknifed across several lanes of freeway scattering its contents on the road. I could see that some of the packages were intended as Christmas gifts, items that would not likely arrive at their destinations.

I knew that I had to avoid the same fate. I had to get to my destination. Diana might be surprised by my unexpected arrival, but I was sure that she would welcome me joyfully once she understood that her greatest potential lay ahead when she stepped off the settled plans she had made with Brian.

The thought of Brian filled me with loathing and some remorse. I had thought of him as a brother at school. But when we had been forced to share the role of soccer captains, everything soured between us. I was surprised he did not just go ahead and do the honorable thing—resign as co-captain, leaving only one of us in charge. He'd thought that sharing the role was the perfect outcome. I remember how he looked at me when the vote was tallied. He told me then, "Albert, you are the best man, no question. That's why I'm so happy to have wound up sharing the role with you." He couldn't have been more pleased.

But I saw only disaster. In the heat of competition, men needed decisive command. They could not be confused by multiple sets of directions. While I could appreciate that Brian saw an opportunity for us to bond as teammates and friends, I saw it for what it really was.

The same had applied to Diana. Brian never seemed to understand what she really needed. He never would understand. Therefore, an almost surgical intervention was necessary, one that would end the future between him and Diana.

I was finally near my destination. Road signs told me the town was five miles away. I knew that a groom's dinner would be starting within the hour, which meant I would have only a crucial few minutes to convince Diana to abandon her marriage plans.

Outside of town, there was a four-way intersection where two highways intersected. I was on the one going east-west. It was heavily patrolled by the local police who often set up speed traps. Signs were posted warning of the traffic change ahead, and speed limits were posted. Given the weather conditions, I decided to hurry through that intersection without stopping since even the slightest pressure on the breaks might cause me to slide and spin. I had so little time to spare, I couldn't afford any delay.

As I was about to pass through the intersection, I noticed a car on the north-south route just starting to cross in front of me. That part of the north-south route came very close to the banks of the river, and a deep embankment fell off the side to the river below.

I pressed the accelerator and hurried through, not looking back to see what had become of the other car. Given the weather conditions and the personal circumstances, I was satisfied that I had made the only decision I could, risky as it was. I couldn't worry about what happened to the other car.

A few minutes later, I pulled up behind Diana's car in her driveway. She had just entered it. I stepped out of my car and walked to hers, rapping on her window.

"What on earth are you doing here?" she asked.

"I need to talk to you right away."

"Albert, I'm on my way to the groom's dinner. Can't it wait?"

"I just need… just a few minutes."

"Five, that's it," she said. "And then I have to go."

She got out of her car and both of us went into her house.

I took her soft hands in mine and looked into her beautiful face, noticing once again the slight flaw. Her eyes were uneven and too close together, almost crossed. I remembered being irritated by how idiotic she could sometimes look, but my irritation was only momentary since I gazed down to see her exceptionally memorable breasts revealed by a low-cut gown. Still, that only made me detest Brian, as I knew that he had nothing but self-interest in mind in wanting that perfect figure next to his.

"You can't marry him," I said in a firm voice.

She drew her hands away. "You have to be joking. You? Coming here after jilting me?"

"I'm completely serious."

"And what makes you say this, after all this time?"

"He's not good enough for you," I said.

"Right. And I suppose you are?"

I considered her question. Yes, I was ideal for her. But the opposite was not true. Not yet at least. I could not be sure until we spent more time together. Again.

"I see," she said. "You have no immediate answer. Right, Albert."

"You misread my hesitation. I was considering everything that has happened since our engagement ended…"

"Since you jilted me, you mean."

"If you will only listen. There's so much, Diana, that you could be. So much more than just…" I could almost not say his name, but I had to "…just Brian's wife."

I could see the tears welling up in her eyes. "So, you're expecting me to rip my heart out again? What on earth are you talking about? Are you saying you want me back again?"

I had to be honest. "Yes. I want to be in your life, Diana."

Tears began to fall down her cheeks.

I had to be more honest. "But not in the way you are thinking. In a better way—where both of us are the persons we need to be."

"I'm confused," she said. "Are you asking me to marry you? Again?"

"Let me try to be clearer," I said, reaching into my pocket for the engraved silver case I always carried with me. I took out my business card and handed it to her.

She read it and looked at me, then began to laugh. All my clients did at first. I was used to it.

"The Emporium of the Future You?" She laughed even harder. "Parque? Are you serious?" She tore the card in half and buttoned her coat.

"I'm leaving now, Albert. I'm leaving to go and see my future husband and his family." She put her hand on the doorknob. "Please leave. I don't ever want to see you again."

A look of surprise came into her face. The door opened from the other side, and there stood her parents.

Diana saw the shock in her parents' faces and responded quickly. "Mom, Dad. Uh, yes… I was as surprised to see Albert as you are. He was just leaving."

"Darling," her mother said, hardly able to speak. The woman had been sobbing before the door had opened. I was taken aback by the reaction I was getting from Diana and now her family. "This has nothing to do with Albert."

Just then a police car pulled into the driveway behind my vehicle.

"Mom?" Diana asked. "What's going on?"

Diana's mother collapsed into sobs.

Her father finally spoke. "There's been an accident. A terrible accident. Please, let's all go inside and talk."

Diana's mother took her arm gently and walked her inside. Moments later I saw Diana in her father's arms moaning loudly and repeating one word. "No."

I was the only one left at the door when the police arrived on the steps. "Can I help you officer?" I asked, unfailingly polite as always.

"We're looking for the driver of that car," he said, pointing to my car in the driveway.

"That's me," I said. "Albert Parque."

I was handcuffed almost immediately.

"What is this? Let me go," I said. "What am I being accused of?"

"You are under arrest for the vehicular homicide of two people."

"That's ridiculous. I did no such thing," I complained loudly. "Who are you talking about?"

"The intersection just outside of town. A witness identified you and your car speeding through the intersection without stopping."

Suddenly I understood. The car I had seen going through the intersection! I thought it had looked familiar. Then I remembered the faces in the front seat.

Brian and his mother, Mary.

"Three people were headed to a groom's dinner," the officer explained. "The father of the groom, who was in the backseat, saw you speeding through the intersection. The groom was driving and his mother was sitting next to him. They couldn't stop for you and slid through the intersection. Their car plunged down the embankment and the father just barely made it out before the car sank. The young man and his mother were not so lucky."

"But I had to keep driving," I said. "It's not my fault."

No one was listening to me. I wondered if anyone ever would, no matter how convincing my words were. The Emporium of the Future You would never reach its full potential. Albert Parque died that day, and that was the tragedy that no one would ever fully understand—not Diana or her parents. Not Brian's father, who sued me every way he could.

I never spoke to any of them again except through my lawyers.

* * *

As I think about that night—it was so many years ago—there is still so much I do not remember. But I know that I do not wish to compromise myself, even now. I still believe that I have always spoken only the truth, that I told everyone truthfully what I had seen and endured, and what my hopes were for their lives.

I stand now in front of these graves only because of the conditions of my parole. I am forced to come here on a daily basis to try and restore my memory, to recall things I'd rather remained forgotten.

I am not, however, required to bring the objects I carry with me in my satchel. Each time, I leave one more item next to each of tombstones because the ones I left on the last visit have always vanished before I returned.

I run my finger over the engraved lines of my business cards and touch the engraved letters on the tombstones. Will I never be understood? I lay another business card in front of each tombstone, hoping to elicit some response, some recognition from the spirits that may reside here. I wish they would come and take away something useful from these things so I would not be compelled to carry them and their memories everywhere I go, even into my fractured sleep. Do they mean anything to the poor souls buried here? Why is it that objects are so filled with memories yet so unyielding of forgiveness?

Part 3: Denials

Chapter 21—Dead End Relationship

I had never intended to retire so early, but due to a small detail beyond my control, I cannot reinstate my license and am therefore prohibited from medical practice. This is a terrible waste of skill and expertise that today's society really cannot afford. I am as robust at sixty-five as I was at twenty. Now, my steady hands, which I perfected through thousands of complicated procedures, remain idle.

My years of experience flawlessly executing even the most complicated neurosurgeries brought me patients as well as physicians from all over the world who looked on in the gallery while I sorted through the complicated neurosystems of the human cranium. One false move and I could turn a saint into a criminal. A single tremor of my hand could sever all memories. With an errant blink of an eye—causing me to act a split second late—I could accidentally eradicate a patient's entire encyclopedia of emotions. But time and time again, my skill and precision prevented these types of cataclysms, which lesser surgeons might inevitably cause.

In my heyday, I performed as many as five hundred operations per a year, each one with life or death consequences. In one case, I separated Siamese triplets joined at the skull. One wrong move could have doomed the fragile trio. The trickiest part of the procedure was that each child needed to be placed into hypothermic arrest during which all the blood was pumped from their bodies. Then, the complicated procedure to separate and re-circuit their tangerine-sized brains needed to be completed in less than an hour.

Many would have panicked under such pressure, fearful that the slightest wrong move would jeopardize a life, or all three. But I was prepared for everything, even the fact that those assisting me might panic.

This happened to the resident assisting me when we were surprised with an anomaly in one of the children's brains. Blood began squirting out of the child's skull and the startled resident stepped away from the table. I told him, "Calm down, just watch me. It's really no more complicated than peeling a juicy orange."

I heard the scolding tone of the head surgical nurse, but I ignored her. Honesty was always best under these circumstances.

I showed the resident how to peel off the tissue, carefully lift the rest of the bone, take a piece of muscle fascia, and sew it over the defect. Something big had gone wrong, that was true, but it was not a big deal because we were ready for anything. I knew what we were going to do before it happened. No matter how good you are at planning, the pressure to perfect never goes away.

If there was one thing I learned from that pressure, it was that as much as I wanted it not to be the case, humility in the operating room was risky. You had to be a dictator to be a good leader. The operating room was no place for uncontrolled democracy, for give and take.

I also learned that there were no miracles unless I made them happened. I knew I was responsible for every patient's welfare. Whether they lived or died or wound up as a vegetable, I was the one whose career was on the line. That's why I knew that only my opinion mattered. I insisted on absolute fealty. I know this made an enemy or two, but I was never concerned about that. We had tiny lives to save, not big egos to massage or feelings to mend. There were personal risks to questioning my absolute authority in the operating room and I made sure everyone on the surgical team knew that.

The one time I stopped to listen to someone else, the consequences were most dire. In fact, this led to my forced retirement, which I continue to dispute with the State Medical Board. I don't want to go into the details of the dispute here, not necessarily because of the confidentiality clause in my agreement with my former employer. It's my wife who has forbidden me from ever talking about it. And while I think she's wrong, I shall forever acquiesce to her wish.

My dear, precious wife.

The two of us met under not terribly auspicious circumstances. I was a resident neurosurgeon in a now-closed hospital when she was admitted to the ER post-concussion. The circumstances of her concussion were curious to say the least. She claimed not to have been assaulted nor have had an accident.

I overheard the attending emergency room physician questioning her on the issue, and the man's lax skills were instantly apparent.

"Ghosts," she said.

"Ahhh," the attending physician quietly nodded, taking note of what she was telling him. A nurse counted her pulse beats.

As I watched the woman lying there bundled under warm blankets, I feared that she might not receive the care she needed. But I knew it wasn't appropriate to rush in and insert myself into her treatment at this stage. I was determined, though, to stay nearby. I could not allow her to come to harm, even though I could hardly see more than her tiny, upturned nose and her long, graceful arm held at the wrist by the attending nurse at her side.

The ER physician did little more probing than to converse with her as if they were at a party. He said, "Go on? You said your head injury was caused by ghosts?"

"It's always the ghosts—pounding in my head. They bring my concussions on." The woman made this admission in a plain, matter-of-fact tone.

She seemed otherwise lucid, that is if a woman claiming ghosts had caused her concussion can be considered lucid. She was conscious, carrying on conversations with the medical staff, though apparently also in touch with beings from another level of consciousness.

But she was under the treatment of the attending ER doctor, a man I had instantly despised. He was a competent doctor, but I am embarrassed to say the man's bedside manner was beyond terrible. He was a retired military physician and insisted on being referred to by his official rank, as his favorite nurse always reminded me.

"Everyone in the armed services is addressed by their rank," the nurse, a bristling young woman, would hasten to inform me if I mistakenly called him doctor.

"The man has been retired from the armed forces for two dozen years now," I said.

She gave me a cross-eyed look and made this edict clear with one word—"Everyone."

Circumstances of my own forced retirement require that I not call the man by his actual name. Therefore, I refer to him here as Captain Anton Zhivago, USN, Ret. I am under a similar restriction in regards his nurse. Here I call her Lara.

Lara looked far less severe than her manners warranted. Though she was long-limbed and had a narrow waist—the woman had the toned legs and arms of an athlete—her bust seemed to strain against her nurse's uniform. I thought she had purposely worn scrubs too small to accentuate this womanly aspect of her physique. Her features were smooth and even, her eyes widely set, her skin acorn brown, and her black hair woven in a densely coiled arrangement.

It was clear that Captain Zhivago thought her the most attractive person he'd ever seen, and it infuriated me to see how he looked at her, a woman young enough to be his granddaughter. They made a very odd-looking couple—the elderly white Captain and the handsome, severe, young black nurse. But to see him look at her with a less than grandfatherly expression was shocking. He had a lusty look in his eye, and I swore that at some point I would find them hidden in a storeroom locked in a tempestuous embrace.

Captain Zhivago had spent many years in the Navy. He was primarily stationed on submarines, and once he'd retired, he had sworn he would never spend another moment entombed underwater. Given the conditions in submerged vessels, his pale skin had remained untouched by the sun for decades. Without the effects of UV rays, he had not developed a wrinkle, even though the man was in his seventh decade. The only clue that the man was older than he appeared showed in a pair of worn lines bracketing his mouth. Lara told me that the man smiled so often that the grooves were permanently etched in his cheeks.

I had the good manners not to point out that he had the appearance of a lecher ready to prey on any female with no regard to age or marital status. It was unseemly to see the look of desire in that old Captain's watery blue eyes.

My future wife, even in her somewhat semi-conscious state, was not unattractive, and Captain Zhivago looked at her with the same love-struck eyes as gazed upon beautiful Lara. I assume my wife took his look to be ordinary doctor's compassion.

"So, you say ghosts caused your injury?" Captain Zhivago asked.

"No," I heard the young woman say. "Not injured."

The Captain excused himself and took Lara aside. Now I felt free to step in and join their conversation.

"We still don't know anything about her," Lara said.

"Nothing?" the captain asked.

"She didn't have any identification on her. And she can't tell us her name," Lara said.

I spoke up at last. "Can't? Or won't?"

"Doctor, really," the captain said. "The patient clearly has amnesia,"

"That's questionable. What would lead you to make that assumption?" I asked, challenging his initial and very flimsy diagnosis. I knew my statement was brash, some might think arrogant. But I feared that the young woman was in immediate peril and Captain Zhivago didn't have the skill and training needed to diagnose a hangnail.

This woman obviously needed a physician with my advanced training to determine her course of care. I could only imagine that the captain had hung onto a career as a submarine doctor because once such a vessel was at the bottom of the sea, there really was no option to substitute another more competent doctor to attend the naval personnel. They were stuck with him, as incompetent as he was.

"Doctor," the captain said. "Would you like to examine her yourself and let me know what your judgment is?"

Lara had a haughty look. "He's barely been here for a few weeks," she remarked. "This is completely against protocol to allow such an untested person to attend. Are you sure it's wise?"

The captain turned his watery eyes on Lara, the look sickening me once again. The creases at the side of his mouth deepened. "I have confidence in Dr. Park," he told the nurse. "Of course, I'll be right here as well, but I'm certain he will make an accurate judgment as to this patient's needs." Captain Zhivago motioned toward the patient, whose eyes were still closed.

I wheeled a chair toward her bedside, removed a pencil from my breast pocket, and sat down.

Chapter 22—Ghosts

"Miss," I said gently, looking down at the patient to get my first close look at the woman who would soon become my wife. Searching for consciousness, I saw her pupils wavering between sleep and awareness. Her tiny face was crumpled like a tissue against the pillow, pale as the hospital sheets, but her cheeks were rosy from the warmth of either a fever or the warmed blankets piled on top of her.

The diagnostic machines showed her body temperature was normal, her pulse calm, her blood pressure slightly low but within the normal range. There was no physical evidence of whatever ailment required her presence in the ER.

Her hair color was strange, to say the least. That is to say that it was almost transparent, colored platinum white or an eerie see-through gray, I wasn't sure which. Though there was much of it, fanned out all around her on the pillow, it was the finest hair I had ever seen, threadlike as spider's silk.

"I'm Albert Park, M.D." I told her. "I've been asked to evaluate your condition."

For the first time, she opened her eyes. I noticed a detail that hadn't made its way into her chart. Her eyes, a faded shade of gray, seemed lit on places and beings not visible to the ordinary eye, visiting a realm only she could perceive.

"Excuse me a moment," I said to the woman, "I'll be right back." I walked close to Lara and the captain.

"The woman's blind?" I whispered to them.

"Yes," Lara said.

"Why is this fact not listed on her chart?" I asked.

"Why would you expect it to be there, she's only just arrived," the captain said.

"It's obvious anyway," Lara huffed. She pointed to the white cane leaning against the wall along with the patient's other meager belongings—a few Braille books and a dark pair of glasses.

Turning to Lara, I said, "With the little we know about this patient, we can't make judgments at this point as to which details are *obvious*. Nothing can be ignored."

I didn't bother to remind her that she and the captain had already been quite slipshod in their evaluation. They had ignored obvious signs of the patient's need for expert care, paid attention to unessential details, and disregarded important aspects of her presenting symptoms. Thank goodness I had arrived on the scene at just the right time.

I went back to the patient's bedside.

"I'm very thirsty," the woman said, and instantly Lara was there with a glass of ice water and a straw.

I took the glass from her. "Let me help," I said, guiding the patient's hand to the straw. I helped support her head as she leaned forward and sipped.

"Please let me know if you would like more," I said. "I'm here to help you and answer any questions you have. But first, may I ask you a few? We need to better understand what brings you to the emergency room today." I helped make her more comfortable, adjusting her pillows and elevating the bed so she was sitting more upright.

She waited patiently and smiled slightly for the first time.

"Can you tell me who you are?" I asked, thinking I heard a scolding click from Lara who stood just a few feet behind me.

"I wish," she said, her eyes still sightlessly searching the room as if she too was looking for her own identity.

"What do you remember about the past day? And what brought you here?"

"I'm not even sure," the woman began. "I was… was at a bus stop, sitting on the bench. I heard, in the distance, the sound of a departing bus. I might have just gotten off, I don't know."

Small beads of sweat formed on her upper lip.

"Were you alone?" I asked. "There at the bus stop?"

"No." she said.

"Who was there with you?" My voice was growing quieter and quieter. I had the sense that speaking too loudly, too forcefully, would frighten her back into that semi-conscious state she had drifted in and out of.

"They were there," she said. "As always." She seemed to be hinting at some half-remembered history.

"Always?"

"They were so familiar, the way they knew me. I know it sounds strange." The patient's voice grew stronger, and I watched closely to see that she wouldn't strain herself trying to explain. "I mean, I can't remember what happened before I was at the bus stop, but they were with me, as always. It seemed like they knew me."

"Are they here? Did they bring you to the hospital?"

"Yes. They were concerned. One of them, the younger one, practically a child really, held my hand. The other one carried my things."

"Where are these people who brought you to the hospital? We'd like to speak to them."

A smile spread across her face. "I'm not the one to ask, of course." She chuckled as if she'd just heard a joke. "Wouldn't it be better to just ask them yourself?"

"Dr. Park," the captain said, motioning me to step outside the room. I reluctantly excused myself and followed the captain to the corridor.

"Have you heard enough to form a diagnosis?" the captain asked me. Lara was once again giving me a strange look.

"Excuse me?" I said, trying to contain my temper.

"It's obvious that we need to have a psychologist evaluate this young woman," Lara said.

"Obvious?" I asked. To the captain and Lara, everything seemed obvious.

"The woman is showing all the signs of a psychogenic fugue state," the captain said. "Doesn't that seem patently clear?"

Of course, I knew the type of condition the captain was talking about. The kind of malady so frequently suffered in soap opera dramas or dime store novels that one might think it was as common as a head cold.

"I'm shocked you'd actually think so," I said. "That's a rare condition, and while it's true that this woman has its characteristic amnesia, we haven't completely ruled out organic issues, the kind that might be surgically corrected."

The nurse gave me another scolding look. "It seems drastic to be considering surgery at this point, Doctor."

"I completely agree with the nurse," the captain said. "Let's take a look at what we know so far. First, she can't tell us who she is. Second, her memories are missing. Third, she appears to have been wandering, possibly traveling. And fourth, there is no apparent physical trauma. Yet to be determined is the stressor that brought on this condition. I would not be surprised if there were several underlying psychological issues, perhaps an acute, or even chronic, mental illness of some kind. Has anyone checked the psychiatric facilities in the area to see if anyone is missing?"

After listening patiently to the captain, I finally said, "I am of course not ruling out anything at this point. I've barely begun to examine the woman." I gave a stern look at Lara. "I am appalled that not even the most basic information about her has made it into her charts. Please see that it doesn't happen again."

"Yes," Lara said, agreeable at last. "I apologize for the oversight."

"Now, if you will excuse me, I'd like to continue my evaluation." I knew I sounded arrogant, but it seemed required, given the circumstances. The captain was practically sleeping on the job, and Lara was doing nothing to challenge him.

The captain nodded.

I returned to the patient's bedside. She had once again fallen asleep, so I gently woke her. "I hope you don't mind if I ask you a few more questions?"

She yawned prettily, saying, "Of course."

"You mentioned ghosts. A younger one. Tell me more about who brought you here."

"Ghosts," she said, stirring from a light sleep. She smiled a wan smile, then her faded gray eyes opened and focused on a space behind me. I saw a moment of sadness pass through them. "Yes."

"Are these…" I paused, trying to find a different, more present way to refer to the spectral beings that seemed so apparent only to her. But giving up, I finally said, "Are these ghosts you know well? Or maybe *knew* well?" Perhaps people from your life who have passed on?" I searched for words to describe this world beyond science. "Or are they completely unknown to you?"

"Oh, they are very familiar to me," she said, more awake now, her blind eyes more focused. "I have a feeling that I knew them very well before they passed on. They were very dear to me. Very dear." Her voice broke and I saw tears form in her eyes.

I could see that the passing of these individuals had caused her much sorrow. I grew more curious to know who they were. But I knew I must remain patient if I was to unlock what lay hidden in this woman's lost memories.

I then saw her grimace and quickly lift her hands to her temples. "Oh, my head is pounding again."

I hesitated to give her anything for her pain, fearing that she'd fall asleep and be unable to tell me more about the causes of her condition. I did, however, ask if she wanted some pain medication and explained the potential side effects.

She accepted a few children's aspirins, claiming that anything stronger would have even worse consequences. I darkened the room for her and helped her lie back into her pillows, telling her to close her eyes for a few moments.

She did as I asked, but said she needed to keep talking about the ghosts. Talking about them helped her remember them. That was the only possible way her suffering would cease.

I told her I was ready and willing to listen for as long as she needed me. I was at the end of my shift but told the captain and the nurse I planned to stay on voluntarily to care for this patient. I excused the captain and Lara, telling them I would thoroughly examine the patient and provide them with a full report later.

They left, not entirely comfortable with my plan. But there were many other patients in the ER requiring attention.

My patient shivered, her brow wrinkled in pain, and I thought it best to close the door to see if a calmer environment would help her. I dimmed the light even more and sat quietly next to her bedside waiting for her to continue her story.

Chapter 23—Forget-Me-Not

Every time I think about that very first conversation I had so many years ago with the young lady who was to be my wife, I remember how delusional everyone thought she was. It makes me bitter, even angrier than I was that day. Many years have passed, but the thought of how the captain and Lara immediately classified her as mentally unstable makes me rage inside. I can barely speak of those two without shaking.

The captain was seen by many as a fatherly authority who only had the patient's best interests in mind. Cold, clinical Lara was revered for her nursing skills and was seen as a crack diagnostician by everyone but me. Despite their reputations, they had made an immediate judgment and instantly condemned this patient, considering her fit only for an asylum. Why wasn't there the least protective instinct in them? Why didn't they withhold judgment if even for another fifteen minutes?

I also had doubts about her sanity, yet I alone remained objective. I was careful to judge whether I held the opposite viewpoint because the others were reaching their diagnosis on such flimsy evidence. I concluded that my position was the only correct one. And while I also knew that my personal passion was already engaged, I was doubly sure that I had to withhold my medical judgment even longer and give this patient more than the benefit of the doubt.

I knew I was walking a very fine line, that my professional judgment could be easily impaired because I was instantly captivated—not only by her presenting symptoms, but by her beauty and her gentle way of speaking. It was hard not to be. I was already falling under her sway—falling, in fact, in love with her, even thought she was definitely not my usual type. I preferred the more robust, athletic type, and she was not at all hardy. Her physical delicacy went beyond the mere fact of her blindness, which seemed to be not much of a handicap at all, I was to learn. She had an unhealthy pallor, and she was so insubstantial that she seemed practically a ghost herself. But her blindness and her apparent physical flaws hid the truth about her. They were camouflage for her true nature. Her fragile physique was illusory, which I soon learned when more of her story was revealed to me.

Yes, she was as delicate as those tiny alpine flowers, the kind that grow only at the highest elevations. But that makes them hardier than all the other flowers, given the inhospitable, often frigid conditions and lack of oxygen at such heights. For a thing to thrive in such a merciless environment requires supernatural gifts.

This is what all physicians learn but many forget. You cannot accept things at face value. You must always remain open to learn the truth that lies hidden within, to look for the paradox. There were many truths hidden within this patient, this beautiful, frail-looking woman who seemed to have lost all connection to who she was.

I watched her rest, her tiny veins visible in her temples like small lavender-tinged fractures on a fine porcelain cup. I decided to call her "Forget-me-not," naming her after those stubborn, tiny alpine flowers. She didn't have a known name, and that one seemed as good as any, perhaps better than most given the nature of her medical condition.

I waited for perhaps an hour until she finally opened her eyes again and told me that much of her pain had gone away.

"The ghosts?" I asked. "Are they gone now too?"

"No," she said. "They never leave me."

"Didn't you say that the ghosts cause your symptoms—the intense pain?"

She nodded.

"Then, wouldn't it be better if they weren't around?" I asked as gently as possible.

"No," she said, this time without a tear. "That would be the worst possible thing. And I've caused them far more pain then they have ever caused me. I have caused them unbelievable grief. If I suffer in order for them to remain close to me, then I will go on suffering as long as it takes."

How she was so sure of this need, I did not know.

She immediately spoke more on the same topic. "I know. I can tell by your silence that you're surprised by how certain I sound. A woman who cannot remember who she is, where she belongs. One who clings to ghosts. But I'm very sure. They are my only connection to the person I once was, the life I used to lead."

"These ghosts," I said. "Tell me everything you understand about them."

She sat up in her bed suddenly, her eyes wide with fear. She gave a small cry, then covered her mouth saying, "No, no," as if possessed, consumed by a sudden panic.

She felt around the bed with frantic movements and got herself out of the bed so quickly she nearly fell. I stooped to help her, but she was already scrambling across the floor, then feeling along the wall until she had located her things.

"Miss," I said, "What are you doing?"

"They're leaving. I need to hurry if I'm going to keep up with them."

"But you aren't well enough to be discharged," I said. A madness seemed to have suddenly descended upon her. I knew I should call for help, but I was afraid she would be instantly carted off to the asylum, and that would be the last I would see of her.

I glanced outside her room to see if anyone had noticed the commotion, but all was quiet. I turned to see that she had begun to dress, not aware that I was even there. She removed her hospital garment with little concern for modesty. I averted my eyes, but not before noticing how perfect her tiny body was, her skin smooth as a worn stone, her limbs supple though slender, her bosom and hips still girlish, though she was clearly older than I had first thought from her face. I knew then that she had been loved—and she had loved. Without any modesty, she put her street clothes back on.

She had misbuttoned her worn, plaid work shirt but seemed not to care. She buckled oversized denim overhauls, the snapping of the metal buckles sounding like two quick gunshots. Next, she sat on the floor and felt around for her shoes, then pulled on her heavy laced work boots with thick soles, expertly tying them. She was swimming in all of the oversized clothes, which looked like they might have been discards from a charity bin. Lastly, she pulled on a hand-knit wool beret, the only feminine article of clothing she seemed to possess. She felt her way back to the hospital bed and in her hurry knocked everything off the side table except what she sought, her dark glasses.

"I'm going," she said. "I don't want them to leave me here alone." She grabbed her cane and a heavy messenger bag that probably contained all of her possessions.

She proceeded out of her room, and no one seemed to take notice of the woman tapping her cane along the hallway. It was late. The captain and Lara were nowhere to be seen. I knew that it was around the dinner hour, so they were probably off in the cafeteria together as always.

Though my shift had long been over, I decided that I couldn't let Forget-me-not wander off on her own, even though she could discharge herself. I hurried to keep up with her.

"Let me come with you," I said, taking her arm. "At least get you safely outside the hospital." She allowed me to take her heavy bag and I slung it over my shoulder quickly.

"Please don't let them get away," she said.

"I don't even know who you are referring to," I said as I clasped her hand around my arm. "I can't see anyone." I had to admit the truth to her. The corridor was empty. Still, she did not stop. She swept us through the long hallways of the hospital, and I did my best to keep her from running into walls and doors as she followed her unseen companions through the corridors.

She moved quickly and without delay, directed by a compass deep within her, perhaps next to the repository that contained all of her tormented history, the past she'd forgotten but troubled her so greatly it urged her to decisive action. I guided her around obstacles—a janitor's bucket, empty gurneys, deserted nurse stations. My credentials allowed her entrance through restricted areas, making it look as if I was the one leading her and not the opposite. No one suspected anything was amiss.

Orderlies nodded at me as we whisked through the geriatric wing. We made our way through the cardiac area in complete silence, and our steps were matched by the quiet beating of heart machines, the passageway lit only by their pulsating gauges. Occasionally, we were seen by a patient, a nurse, and attending physicians, and it was clear they were struck by the sight of my oddly dressed young companion. But no one seemed to look long at her strange clothing. I noticed that everyone who saw us searched her face, but the blind young woman seemed not to notice any of the living we passed by. Clearly, all of her thoughts were on the spectral presence that she alone could sense.

She paused briefly before stepping into the maternity ward, and I was the one who hurried ahead at the pace she had set, pulling her along. She began to drag behind me.

"Don't move so fast," she said. "They are taking their time in this place." She panted, and I could see sweat forming on her face. I was thankful that she had slowed down but was not sure exactly why.

"Where are we?" she said.

"In the hospital maternity ward."

A wary look passed her eyes. Then, the piercing sound of a newborn wailing from a delivery room stopped her cold. She shuddered and clutched herself, doubled over as if in great pain. I helped her to a deserted lounge and sat her down in a chair.

She seemed unable to breath. Her back arched in pain. She leaned her head against the chair, her hair cascading over the back of the chair, her face contorted with tremendous, concentrated effort. Then, as quickly as the spasm came, it passed.

A look of calmness washed over her face. She said, "We can rest here a moment? Undisturbed?"

I said, "Yes of course," and knowing she planned on staying there, I quickly fetched a glass of water for her.

She drank greedily, and then sat quietly for a moment. Suddenly, she looked at me. Blind though she was, it was as if she was seeing me for the very first time.

"Albert," she said with suffering evident in her voice. "I know you, don't I?"

"I don't think so. We've only just met, in the emergency room a few hours ago." I wanted to comfort her in some way, but I had to be truthful. "We really don't know each other, not yet anyway."

"Oh," she said. "I was so sure that we knew each other. Very well."

Then she began to look angry and cold. Her line of sight, or perhaps insight, directed itself at a chair across the room.

"Yes, of course," she said to the empty chair, speaking as if in conversation with another person. "You knew he would say that."

Then she turned to me and said, "I am told that we know each other very well." Her expression wavered between confusion and disappointment. She appeared to expect the worst.

I wanted to tell her that we would, indeed, come to know each other very well in the years to come. She seemed to want assurance that we were already well known to each other. Before I could say anything else, she reached out for me, her hands finding first my shoulder, then my face.

As she was gathering knowledge of me with her fingers, she turned to look again at the empty chair across the room but clearly addressed me, saying, "Tell me again whether we know each other or not."

I had to be complete in my answer, as truthful as I could possibly be. It had never mattered more than this very moment, so I took some time to carefully consider her question from every angle.

Perhaps our standards of "knowing" each other were very different. She was, after all, apparently suffering from some form of amnesia. Whether that was brought on by a traumatic physical or emotional event was not yet known. She was, in a way, almost newborn in memory. Therefore, she had known me for all of the existence of her memory, which had really begun only this morning.

I had very high standards when it came to what was an intellectual evaluation of the depth of a relationship. Because of these standards, my social circle was very small. I was acquainted with many people, and many were acquainted with me, and while some would say that they knew very well who I was—and would state that in a dismissive tone—I knew that they had made a snap judgment that was completely wrong. How could anyone know, really, how my thinking worked? I knew that my methods and thought processes were very different from the average person. Was there any way another person could actually understand the mind of a man with the capacity for ground-breaking thought that I was? My mind had a foreign way of thinking, which was easier to ridicule than to understand.

With Forget-me-not, I had a chance, a real chance, of being understood, perhaps for the first time. She had no preconditioned judgment. I also suspected that her condition was reversible, most likely by surgery. I was eager to help her become cured from her memory loss and had several experimental techniques in mind. So, not only was it possible for someone to truly come to know me—without being informed by preconceived notions—but by working with her as a patient, I had a chance of engineering her, making it possible for her to learn about me objectively in a proper way. I could actually see myself making her mind a fertile, flexible place that would bring her years of beautiful service and gratitude.

"Do we?" she asked again, one hand feeling my eyes and brows, the other hand near my mouth. She would have sensed any quiver, any judgment, her fingers were so sensitive in their light exploration of my face. "Tell me whether we know each other," she said.

"As much as I want to give you an answer that might ease your suffering, I have to be completely honest." I said. "And while I certainly want to know you, and be known by you, as no one else in your life knows you, I have to tell you that no, we do not know each other at all."

Her hands fell to her lap, her head sunk, and she wept in disappointment, alone and forsaken. I couldn't help her with a lie, the one she seemed to so desperately want to hear. But I would do everything in my power to heal her, knowing that I could not give her the one thing she so desperately wanted. I would go on to perform many miracles in neurosurgery but would never be able to give her the one thing she wanted more than anything in the world—my memory of her. I could not give her the past that she was certain she had but simply didn't exist.

I said it a third time, just so there would be no further misunderstanding. I knew the worst thing I could possibly do was apologize for myself. I had to state the fact. Only with the truth could one be set on the path to healing.

"I don't know you at all, Miss."

Chapter 24—Lethe

Late in my life, I began to take a keen interest in classical mythology. I read Homer, Bulfinch's Mythology, even comic books if they gave me insights I couldn't find elsewhere. I became a regular at the local comics store, a tiny shop in a strip mall a thirty-minute bus ride from my apartment. I had to pace myself to make sure I arrived just a few minutes after the shop opened for business each day, as the usual customers always hung out in front of the store, sometimes for an hour or more, to discuss their favorites. It was always the same conversation—actually more of a multi-voice monologue—a lot of freaks stammering loudly to no one in particular on a sidewalk in an industrial part of town.

I'll be honest. I know I didn't look terribly different from the usual clientele, which came in all shapes and sizes, and it was not unusual for the customers to be socially awkward, alternating from over-friendliness to sullen silence. I fell into either camp—depending upon the mood of the shop owner. If he seemed the least bit affable and open to discussing my particular interest, then I could spend an hour chatting with him. If he was in his typical stand-offish mood (the man could be churlish), then I kept to myself.

I knew I could be quite exacting, and I was always looking for very particular information. After an extensive search, I located a series that gave me what I was looking for—detailed maps and descriptions of the underworld ruled by the god of the dead, Hades. I'm not sure what fascinated me so much about the underworld, but I continued to be driven to get my hands on as much literature as I could find about it. I even begun to take up a study of Greek, in order to delve into as many original texts as I can locate. But not many are located, so I make do with comics.

I was at a standstill in my profession. I was, for the most part, alone all day long except for the occasional conversation with a cashier or a waitperson. My days were very long indeed. At times they seemed endless. So, I escaped by reading about places beyond comprehension. It helped to have full-color, detailed illustrations of the Greek world of Marvel comics. When I found a well-drawn illustration in a comic book, I cut it out and discarded the rest. Each picture I found I added to the mural of Hades I was creating on the largest wall of my room. I assembled the pictures as if I was creating a jigsaw puzzle of the netherworld.

The Hades realm was a strange landscape to be sure, even though it contained both fields and rivers. I learned in my study that of the five rivers in the classical Greek underworld, there was one with waters that offered rebirth. The other four, the river of sorrow (Akheron), the river of hate (Styx), the river of lamentation (Kokytos), and the river of fire (Phlegethon), all barred the way to peace in the afterlife. It was only through drinking the water of Lethe, the river of forgetfulness, that one could be cleansed of all connection to one's previous life. It was said that Lethe borders Elysium, the final resting place of the virtuous. Apparently, forgetfulness was an essential ingredient to virtuousness, at least in the classical Greek mind. This still seemed very odd to me. Wasn't it more heroic, more virtuous, to have a chest full of medals, souvenirs (i.e., memories) of a lifetime of valor? Proof of one's virtue and sufficient evidence to permit you passage into blissful eternity? Why was it necessary to forget a virtuous earthly life to be admitted to a virtuous afterlife?

An alternate viewpoint came to me one sleepless night, in which I tossed and turned for no apparent reason. Perhaps that oblivion brought on by the waters of Lethe had less to do with forgetting and more to do with forgiving. I was told how central forgiveness was to health, and I know this was true even though the world had never been terribly forgiving or understanding to me.

I thought more and more about Lethe, about oblivion, than ever. Remembering those early days with the young woman I hoped would become my wife, I could think of nothing else.

Forget-me-not and I sat together in the maternity ward of the now-closed hospital where I was a resident neurosurgeon many years ago. Though she was completely blind, she had led me through the corridors as if the opposite were true, as if I was the blind person in need of her sighted guidance. Visions I could not see led her and I was the follower. I know the story sounds completely backward and confusing. In addition to her blindness, she had some form of memory blindness, an unusual kind of amnesia. She had just told me point blank that she was certain we knew each other very well. And I had denied her statement. Now she began again to have an unspoken conversation with a ghost who she claimed was leading us through the hospital corridors.

Occasionally we would hear the sharp cry of a newborn, and at first these sudden sounds caused her to visibly shudder, sometimes reacting as if there was a deep, stabbing pain from within her, the kind of pain a woman has when giving birth. I had studied the mind in great detail when I was learning my profession, and it was clear to me that her pain wasn't "real," it was what some might call "psychosomatic," though I did not believe there was any science connected with that theory. A physical illness brought on by a thought process, in effect, inorganic causes, was an idea totally foreign to my way of thinking.

Take, for example, the ulcer, once thought to be exclusively caused by mental and emotional stress. For years we tried to treat ulcer patients by getting them to relax or do yoga. Finally, it was "discovered" that ulcers do indeed have an organic origin—bacteria. While there continued to be dispute as to whether the bacteria's effect was heighted by stress, the end result is that in not treating the actual cause of the problem, the problem continued.

I believed that mental illnesses were always organic and never emotional nor spiritual in nature, and that surgery was the only viable option for discovering and correcting mental wounds that impaired thinking.

Still, with Forget-me-not, I marveled at how one person could have so much empathy to the suffering all around her. After telling her I didn't know her, for a while she was quiet, almost mournfully so, even though occasional cries sounded from somewhere within the numerous rooms.

"If you would," I said, trying to engage Forget-me-not in conversation once again, "please talk to me. Tell me what the ghost is saying. Who it is."

Even though everything she talked about illustrated that she was on the edge of insanity, I knew I had to keep her talking, if only to connect her to the real world—somehow coax her back into it.

Her face grew even paler than it had been. "Ghosts," she said.

I was relieved that she had finally begun to speak again. "How many are there?"

"Two," she said. "A young child, a boy. An older man. It's the child who brought us here."

"Here to the maternity ward?"

"Yes. He remembers being born here."

That was a remarkable statement. Not only did young children lack the skills to form memories—most did not have memories before their third or fourth birthday—but this ghost child remembered being born. I had learned one thing from this exchange. The younger ghost was a boy.

"Tell me more about the child," I said, coaxing her, glad to hear her voice stronger than it had been the entire time I'd known her, even though what she related grew more fantastical.

"He said you were here. At his birth."

Her unseeing, faded gray eyes were on my face, searching for something I couldn't fathom. Recognition? Her look was so resolute that I began to search my own memories. Had I perhaps been called to the maternity ward for a neonatal consult? I'd been at the hospital for a few years. I'd seen many patients and had been called to many parts of the hospital for consultations on any number of cases. I had yet to perform my most intricate procedures, such as the one separating the conjoined triplets. But I was beginning to be known for my skill, so it was not unusual for me to be asked for my opinion.

"I'm sorry," I replied. "I'm just not recalling any specific memory of attending a birth recently. How old is the boy?" I knew this sounded strange.

She looked at a vacant chair and held up her hands to show an age. Five fingers on the right and the thumb on the left.

"He's six?" I asked.

"Yes."

Had I attended a birth six years earlier?

"Here?" I asked.

"Yes."

"What else does he tell you? What else does he remember?" I didn't point out that the only intact memories of this event were courtesy of a boy ghost. Neither Forget-me-not nor I knew of the event.

She began to relate in great detail the story of the boy's birth. Giving me the story in bursts, she translated to the present world what the departed young spirit told her.

BOY GHOST, as translated by Forget-me-not (BOY): a six-year-old ghost.	ALBERT PARK, M.D. (A.P.), a brilliant young neurosurgeon.
BOY: It was very warm and dark, but I couldn't breathe. Mommy would not talk to me anymore.	A.P.: Where are you?

BOY: I am still inside Mommy. But she's not talking any more. I'd been hearing the shush-shush of her, all around me, like a calm breeze. The thump-thump of her heart. Sometimes the gurgle of her stomach.

A.P.: So this is before you were born?

BOY: Yes. But some of the hospital people are trying to make Mommy talk again and she won't.

A.P.: *Silent*

BOY: The others are reaching inside for me, but I don't want to come out. I'm hiding. It's safe inside Mommy, even though I can't breathe.

A.P.: But you must come out. Whether you want to or not?

BOY: Yes. I am finally brought out. It's cold and bright. Everyone is wearing face masks, blue clothes. I'm surrounded by blue ghosts, all of them coming after me with towels and hospital things. They are stabbing my arms, wiping my face. I'm scared. I'm screaming.

A.P.: They are the attending doctors in the delivery room. They are only trying to help you.

BOY: It's frightening, but I finally calm down. A man is holding me, looking at me.

A.P.: *Shaking uncontrollably, not sure why.* May I ask a question?

BOY: Yes.

A.P.: *Still shaking violently.* Who is the man holding you After you're born?

BOY: My father. Everyone all around him is saying "Sorry. Sorry." They keep saying "Sorry."

A.P.: *Now with tears running down my face.* Why this violent reaction? Why are they sorry?

BOY: Mommy has passed away.

A.P.: *Moaning, arms around me, rocking in disbelief.*

I don't know how long I sat there, crying uncontrollably as if possessed. Forget-me-not's arms were around me, trying somehow to comfort me. Why was I so bereaved, hearing this tale of Forget-me-not's?

"He has more to tell you," Forget-me-not said quietly when I had at last calmed down. "But not here," she said. "We must leave here for him to tell you more."

I did not want to hear anymore of her delusions. I was coming around to the captain's point of view on Forget-me-not. This was insanity. I still knew that I could cure Forget-me-not, and I was certain that surgery was the only possible course of treatment. I knew I was the only one capable of the type of microsurgery required, which would reach into the sensitive place where the deepest and most traumatic memories were hidden.

But I was in no shape to be performing a complex neurosurgery. There was nothing else I could do but continue to follow Forget-me-not, following these ghosts who claimed to know me very well.

Chapter 25—The Abyss

I learned that the best resource for the study of the classical underworld is to be found in reading Virgil's *The Aeneid*. Publius Vergilius Maro began writing his most famous poem around 30 BCE when he was forty years old. I started out reading a translation, of course, and I'm beginning to study Latin, hoping I can get back to the source and get the truest picture of the underworld. I want to hear the sounds of the poetry, the long and short syllables, the stress-accents. Only the lushness of the original language can convey additional meanings not available in even the best translations.

An epic poem, the *Aeneid*, tells the story of the foundation of the Roman Empire. In it, the half-god hero—son of the Goddess of Love and a mortal father and Trojan war hero—has many adventures as he makes his way from war-sacked Troy to Rome. Among these is a visit to the world that exists beyond death.

Reading the *Aeneid* is never easy for me, and it has nothing to do with my lack of fluency in Latin or the epic poem's absence of illustrations because Virgil wrote his poem in a vivid, almost painterly fashion. I can see and smell the war scenes. I can sense the presence of the gods, their anger, their alternately cavalier and fiercely loving attitudes toward the mortals.

I read and re-read, looking for the answer to a mystery I cannot even articulate. Reading the *Aeneid*, of course, never fails to bring back memories of my first day with Forget-me-not. I know I was no Aeneas. Forget-me-not was no Sybil. But like Aeneas, we were both fated to be exiles—she from her memories and I from everything that came after that fateful day we met.

With each re-reading, I have understood better the longing of the souls denied passage on Charon's boat, the only vehicle that could convey them to their promised reward of the afterlife. Charon turns many more away than he permits passage. It does not matter how just or heroic a life you have led, or how innocent you are at the time of death. Yes, even mothers and newborns can be in the group Charon denies. These are the poor souls who have not yet found a resting place on earth. They are condemned to roam the riverbanks for at least a hundred years, and even then they may not be accepted for a crossing.

"Understand their longing" is perhaps an understatement. It is entirely visceral, completely exquisite, this torment that I seek—like those fervently religious monks who mortify their own flesh with whips, beating themselves bloody as a form of extreme penance. It is in the wave of exquisite, loving grief that I experience the greatest connection to my wife, one that has long since been broken. I know perhaps that it's a form of romantic nostalgia for a time that existed however briefly. This is the mystery I struggle to articulate. It is not exactly mourning, even though I can find myself weeping uncontrollably. It's ecstasy, a drug-free high, even though I am sometimes left whimpering and sobbing, unable to move for hours.

* * *

Forget-me-not took me to the elevator lobby of a hospital long since closed where apparently I was a respected neurosurgeon. We waited for a few minutes of conversation between our ghost escorts. I saw some hesitation in Forget-me-not's eyes, and once or twice she started to walk in the opposite direction from the elevator.

"This is the way out?" she asked the ghost, waiting for clarification. She nodded, then returned to the elevator, understanding what our unseen guides were communicating to her. Even though I knew the exit was in the opposite direction, we all nevertheless got on the elevator. I was not aware whether the ghosts got in or not. I just assumed they did. I sensed a conversation going on around me, one taking place in an otherworldly language I did not speak. I relied on a blind woman to be my translator.

I watched as Forget-me-not felt the Braille numbers on the elevator's floor-selection panel, then pushed the one that took us to the service level of the hospital. I watched the number light briefly, then shut off. When the elevator car had not moved, she pressed it again and the number lit, then went off. Forget-me-not looked briefly puzzled, then turned toward me.

"You have a key," she said. "The boy says that you need to insert the key. The floor is locked, except to hospital personnel."

Without saying it, I thought, Even to ghosts? But the ghosts could not lead the human tourists through solid walls and floors, and the humans could not descend to where the ghosts wanted to lead us unless the elevator would take us there. I was the only one with the power to continue this journey of Forget-me-not.

I did indeed have the key. I briefly considered not unlocking the bottom-most floor. It was sheer lunacy. But next to the woman who was to become my wife, who was deepening my love with each footstep, I was powerless.

I inserted the key next to the button for the lower level, then pressed it and the elevator immediately descended. When we reached our destination, the doors opened, and I stepped onto a floor I'd never previously entered.

Immediately, we were met by a hospital employee I had never seen before but who acted as if he knew me very well. He drove up to us in a small, motorized cart, much like the sky-cabs that transport passengers inside an airport.

"Good evening, Dr. Park," he said without much of a smile. He wore a simple driver's uniform in olive green with a cap that read "Driver." He had a matching jacket, and I could just see the edge of a nametag stitched to his shirt but couldn't see what the man's name was. Though his cap concealed much of his hair, I could see it was silver. His face was markedly smooth for a man with such gray hair, but the narrow creases that marked his cheeks and his wrinkled hands, made it clear that he was somewhere in his late 60s, an age that normally would have required him to retire.

He asked where we needed to be taken. I felt ashamed that even though I was Forget-me-not's treating physician, I didn't know. And I could hardly explain that Forget-me-not, a blind woman, was relying on ghosts for our direction. So, neither of us said a thing.

"Get on," the driver said plainly. "I'll take you where you need to go."

So, we got on, settled on the bench behind the driver's seat, and he drove us along the winding passageway.

We passed by room after room, each one containing a physician, a patient, and perhaps several other medical persons. Many of the patients had festering open wounds that were obviously not healing, broken bones that jutted out from torn skin and looked very much beyond repair, and all manner of rashes and tumors. More than a few of the patients were being given last rites, and I saw robed priests and rabbis scurrying back and forth in front of our vehicle.

The conditions of these treatment rooms were unbelievably unsanitary. I spotted flies and other insects flying and crawling about, garbage receptacles that were overflowing, and unwashed, unsterile instruments that had been reused.

"What is this wing?" I asked. I wanted to add: And why have I never known of its existence until now? But I knew it made me sound ridiculous.

Our driver pulled over and turned around in his seat. I realized then why he had seemed familiar to me. He bore a striking resemblance to my long-deceased father, as he might have looked had he survived to the age of our driver—somewhere around sixty or seventy.

Forget-me-not seemed taken aback by my question.

"I'm sorry if I startled you," I said to her. "I've never been to this wing of the hospital before."

"You see him?" she asked, surprised.

"Yes. Of course." I said. "He's as real to me as you are."

"But not the boy?" she asked.

"Is he still here?"

"Of course. He's next to the driver pointing out the route to take."

"The driver's as real as you are," I said to her. "I'm sorry I can't say that the little boy is, even though you're so certain he exists." Again, I knew my honesty could be too much for her, though I had to admit I really wanted to believe in her.

"The driver," she said, "is the other ghost."

That was the moment the insanity of her world became clear to me. Everything I knew told me not to be convinced there was a ghost driving us through the hospital corridor. But as I remember her face all these years later, how she looked at me in the horrid basement of that defunct hospital, she was the very model of what the truth should be. The truth was embodied in a tiny woman in a heavy plaid work-shirt, oversized denim overhauls and steel-toed work boots wearing a cap that had fallen off more than once.

I know this sounds strange. Everything she told me that day was completely foreign to what I knew and believed about life. Forget-me-knot spoke to ghosts. Though she was an amnesiac, she claimed I knew her when I did not. She told me one of the ghosts had told her that I was present at his birth. Since she had no past she could remember, she also had no motive for making observations that were fanciful rather than factual. She had absolutely no reason to lie.

Yes, I wanted to be convinced by her. But I was the doctor—and she my patient. I had to keep her confidence. It was my only hope of treating and eventually curing her. I did my best to stay on high moral ground. I could not play along with her lie, no matter how guileless she was in telling it to me.

"I'm sorry," I said as gently as I could. "The man is plainly no ghost."

The driver stepped off the cart and asked me to get off as well. "I won't be spoken about in that tone of voice," he said. "And I refuse to drive you any further."

"I apologize, sir," I said to him, wondering what I had done to insult him.

"Do you still not recognize me?" He said, obviously angry and hurt.

"I've never seen you before today," I said. "I never even knew this floor existed. How could I possibly recognize you."

"It's me, son," he said, taking off his hat. "Your father."

Chapter 26—Oblivion

The cart driver stood before me for quite some time as I processed what he was telling me. But it didn't take long for an immediate, unfortunate reaction.

"How dare you claim to be my father," I said.

"Excuse me?" he said. "I should be asking you how dare you be my son? I've been waiting for you for many years—expecting you every day to come visit me like a true son would visit his father. I kept faith in you, even though you ignored me all these years."

"Ignore you?" I was speechless, but not for long. I could not hold back my temper. "You... I mean... My father has been dead for more than twenty years." I rubbed my eyes and blinked. I staggered backward.

The man did look like an older version of the man I remembered. And his gestures, his way of speaking, firmly, quietly—in every way he did, indeed, resemble my father. But the fact was that my father had died many years earlier in a tragic boating accident.

He corrected me, just like my father had done when I was a boy. He took a breath, and the count went on in my head exactly as it had during his life. I heard myself counting five beats, because that is always what my father had preached. Never act rashly. Give yourself time to respond.

"Just because I died doesn't mean you can ignore me," he said. "I continued to believe in you, even though you clearly stopped believing in me long ago. Finally, it looks like you're starting to come to your senses."

That was the last he said on the matter before changing the subject. "Now, this young lady has been patiently waiting for us. She needs us to take her back where she belongs, where she needs to go."

He got back onto the cart. Before driving off, he looked at me once again. "Are you going to join us or not?" He spoke exactly how my father would have, in a not quite scolding tone but clearly indicating his patience had limits.

Then I saw the marks. One mole, like a small comma, marked his right cheek. I touched my own face, knowing that I had the same mark in the same place. My thoughts and heart were racing. I was feeling close to collapse, given this man's revelation, and now the unique punctuation mark we both had.

"Wait," I said. "Just another minute. Please." I found a gurney and leaned against it.

He sighed. "I've been waiting long enough. I suppose I can wait."

He watched me panting, the sweat running down my face. I still thought of asking him for some proof, a coherent story that made sense. I don't know, maybe even a birth certificate, some way of proving that he was who he said he was, though I knew asking a ghost to produce paperwork was a ridiculous idea. Even a real man might have difficulty coming up with definitive proof. Then I concluded he would probably react poorly to whatever I asked him. I glanced again at the raised comma on his cheek.

His eyes lit up. "You know," he said. "You haven't changed much." He even laughed a little, and I could see how yellow his teeth were, as grooved and crooked as any old man's teeth might be. He looked about how you would expect an old man, or ghost, to look. Gaunt. Like he didn't really enjoy life's pleasures much anymore. I'd seen it a lot in my elderly patients. They'd try to lose weight for years, then all of a sudden drop forty pounds in a few months. Their taste buds would be shot.

"What makes you say that?" I said to him, my tone more challenging than I knew was wise. But I felt defiant. I saw Forget-me-not shudder, and that was when I regretted my angry reaction.

The man said, "You have that look on your face, just like you did when you were five years old."

I hurriedly tried to compose myself, to hide whatever he might be noticing.

He just laughed and said, "You were always so sure of yourself, even as a boy. Self-righteous, almost. You were unbelievably stubborn and had five or ten temper tantrums a day, your face growing as red as it is now. Look— you even have your hands clenched into fists like you're ready to pound on something, anything, the wall. Me. When you got this way, we had to lock you in your room until you calmed down. Even before you learned to walk. When you got into one of these moods, we'd put you in your crib and let you bawl it out."

Locked in like a prisoner, I remembered.

Then I said, "Tantrums about what?" I could not imagine myself as the person he claimed I'd been. I remembered always been a calm and thoughtful person.

"Goodness. What *didn't* you have a tantrum over? If I gave you a glass of water that was not exactly the temperature you liked—tepid when you wanted cold, with ice-cubes when you wanted it room temperature— then you'd threw a fit. You always reacted as if everyone was out to get you. As if I had given you something on purpose that didn't match your demanding specifications just to mess with you. I guess it's not surprising you wound up in this profession," he said, gesturing with wide open arms.

"What do you mean?" I tried hard to calm down by unclenching my fists and my jaw. The ghost had me where he wanted me, usurping my reality with his trump card of authenticity, speaking from beyond the dead. Did ghosts lie? Who knew? Until that moment I hadn't believed in ghosts, let alone that their version of reality was somehow truer than the cold, hard evidence of the real world.

The man raised his voice and said, "You doctors all have a God complex. I guess that's how deceitful, spoiled brats grow up. Into people with the unshakable belief that they alone are correct, they alone have all the answers, they hold that one privilege over everyone. Science! Medicine! That is not the be-all end-all. Just because something can't be proved with facts and evidence doesn't mean that it isn't true."

I gave in. A ghost could not be reasoned with. My silence answered him just as all my arguments had answered his expectations. I hadn't become what he'd hoped, only what he'd expected, and there was no way of convincing him of anything else.

He continued his harangue. "Like I said, you haven't changed, son. Guess I'm not surprised, but I did not expect to be back in *your* life and see the same Albert all over again. Living in Albert's fantasy world *once* was enough for me. I didn't expect you'd invade my afterlife with the same ridiculous point of view. Let me tell you something, Albert. You won't find peace in the afterlife with that attitude."

I was confused. "Wait. Am I dead?"

"Of course not," my father said. "But I'm not completely sure why you're here. I know that you're a trained medical professional, but I'm not sure how that's going to change anything for this young lady." He nodded toward Forget-me-not. "But you're a visitor. Temporarily." He glanced toward the bench "So get on."

For the first time, I could see the nametag on the man's shirt. *Peter.* My father's name.

My father's occupation in the afterlife was not too different from the one he'd had during his days on earth. He'd been a city bus driver. The clothing he was wearing was not too dissimilar to the olive-green uniform I'd seen him wear every day. He'd just exchanged his city bus for a three-passenger motorized cart. The only thing missing was the fare box, and I would not have been surprised to suddenly notice one. I'd missed so many other signs until this point.

I got on, and just in time to sense the familiar feeling of being judged by my father and coming up short. But there was precious little time for me to work through my feelings about his old, unforgiven grievances with me.

Suddenly, Forget-me-not fell against me, clutching herself in a convulsion of pain. She wrapped her arms around her middle, tensing in great agony.

"Well, we'd better hurry," Peter said, starting off in a jolt.

"Where are we going?" I shouted, holding tight to Forget-me-not with one arm and hanging onto the rickety bench seat with the other.

"You call yourself a doctor?" he said in disbelief. "Where else would we be going? Goodness, what are they teaching people in medical schools these days?"

I looked at him, still confused.

"The woman is in *labor*," he said, exasperated and waving his arms. "We need to get her where she belongs, and fast."

"In labor?" I said. Then I glanced at Forget-me-not, remembering her slender, tiny frame. She'd presented in the emergency room with migraines not more than a few hours ago. Blood tests had been done and I'd seen all the results. Even after all that testing, her diagnosis was a mystery to everyone. The only clear problem was her amnesia.

Now, I looked down at the woman next to me and saw the enormous belly of a pregnant woman. How could she have hidden her pregnancy from everyone, especially me, a physician? Even a doctor as negligent as the captain couldn't have missed it, yet he did.

Indeed, Forget-me-not was pregnant and just moments from delivery.

Chapter 27—Lost

I was not at the height of my powers as a surgeon yet, and Forget-me-not was in a desperate situation, fading in and out of consciousness, obviously in need of medical attention fast. Needless to say, all my training and experience involved the human mind. I'd read exhaustively on every opinion, surgery, theory and hypothesis about what happened inside the skull. I had no experience in obstetrics.

Forget-me-not, led by these ghosts, had already taken us through the maternity ward, and I knew it must be many floors above us. But as Peter drove us through the byzantine twists and turns of the subbasement, we seemed to be driving away from the elevators and deeper into the underground part of the medical complex, if that's where we still were. Was there a shortcut back to the maternity floor, or another maternity suite down here that I didn't know about?

After taking a number of turns and sliding through a series of automatic doors, we entered a long, narrow passageway with no treatment rooms. The walls were full of windows, and even though I thought we were far below the ground, daylight streamed in and I could see a lush forest outside. We must have slowly been ascending, or else I was too distracted in supporting Forget-me-not's intense, late stages of labor. Thankfully, she had fallen into an exhausted sleep and was leaning against me, her head thrown back against my shoulder. She had never looked more beautiful—her cheeks flushed from exertion, the sweat glistening on her skin, her hair tangled in damp curls around her face.

I had never seen a more stunning place. Birds of every color flitted past, their long feathers radiant in iridescent colors I could not name. Lichens of every shade of blue, green and gray covered the tree trunks, and I could smell the damp, humid air of this verdant paradise somehow seeping through the thick glass. It was not the same landscape that surrounded the now-closed hospital, which was situated near the city center and encircled by interstate highways. I wondered if what I was seeing outside the windows was projected somehow like an artist's installation. I wanted to wake Forget-me-not so she wouldn't miss the scenery but decided to let her rest as long as she could. I had no idea how far away the maternity ward was or how near her next contraction might be.

A tiny monkey gaped at me as we sped by a branch where he sat. He was no larger than a man's hand, and his face looked like a war mask with bright red accents around his eyes and fierce designs on his cheeks. When he saw us, he opened his mouth to screech, and while I couldn't hear the noise he made, his intentions were clear. He was trying to frighten us away from his territory. But I was the only one who saw him, unless somehow the little ghost boy sitting next to Peter had also seen him.

Peter began to whistle a nonsensical tune as we drove along, seemingly oblivious to the scenes outside. The sunlight flashed at us like a strobe, hidden and revealed by the thick forest outside the hospital. It hit me full on the face when we passed along a meadow full of blooming mountain flowers, and I tried to block the sun from Forget-me-not's face in the moments that it was at its most intense. I managed to help her stay asleep and wondered how long I could keep her comfortable given the impending birth.

"This is the way to the maternity ward?" I asked, glancing out the window to see that we had come to a rockier terrain that seemed to be at a higher elevation. There we passed over a small stream, which flowed down from a distant mountain, passed beneath the hospital corridor, and fell just beyond the other window over the edge of a precipice and into a deep chasm beyond my view.

"The boy knows the way, thank goodness," Peter said. "Everything would be lost if we had to rely on you for direction."

Chapter 28—Locked Doors

At last, we arrived at the end of the corridor. The last hundred yards of it were windowless, and when we stopped, there was very little outside light left and no electrical lighting at all. A pair of huge industrial doors barred our way. A large sign was posted that read "Authorized Personnel Only." Even if we could get the doors open, the entrance wouldn't be wide enough for the cart.

"Quickly," Peter said, getting out of the cart.

I lifted an unconscious Forget-me-not and carried her to the door.

"The key, you idiot!" My father said, holding out his arms to take Forget-me-not from me.

"You don't have one?" I asked Peter. "You're not 'authorized?'" I wasn't comfortable handing my future wife over to my dead father.

"Are you going to argue with me now? No. I don't have a key. Only you do. Haven't you kept up to date on the policy? Your medical work leaves a lot to be desired, and I guess I'm not too surprised you pay no attention to policy. You never cared much for authority."

Forget-me-not mumbled groggily. I told her not to speak, she needed to save all her strength. But she kept mumbling and began to struggle in my arms.

"Before you drop her, let me take her," my father said, his gaunt arms held out.

"Let me go!" Forget-me-not said. She was in the grip of yet another contraction. They were coming one after another. I held her out to my father, reluctantly putting her into his arms. I watched for a moment to be sure he was holding her securely.

She moaned and I saw a look of devoted tenderness on my father's face. I could not imagine looking at Forget-me-not in any other way. Then he glanced at me with a look of urgency. I could see that fear was overwhelming his orneriness.

I searched my pocket for the key but came up with nothing. I patted down the chest pockets of my coat and still wound up empty. Where had my keys gone?

"Good gracious, son," father said. "Now what? Have you lost them?"

"I know I put them back in my pocket at the elevator," I said, feeling in my pockets again.

I hurried back to the cart, barely able to see anything. I felt around on the seat where I had been, the floor beneath it. I pushed my hands as far under the seat as I could, tearing the skin around my knuckles and jamming my fingers in the process. I ignored the pain, knowing that Forget-me-not was in far worse shape than I was. I admitted to myself for the first time that day that she was close to death, even though this seemed impossible. She was going to be my wife—but we hadn't even become engaged yet. How could she be dying?

I returned to my father's side. "I can't find them anywhere. I know I had them."

"Look again," he demanded. "Search the place again… where they should be."

I retraced my steps. Felt every part of the cart—where I had been sitting, where Forget-me-not had sat, even where my father had sat. There was only one more spot I hadn't checked. The place where the little boy ghost had been sitting next to my father. But the keys were not to be found.

Forget-me-not appeared to fall in a coma.

"I'm sorry," I whispered in shame. "I can't find the key." My lips brushed against her feverish cheeks.

I heard a tap on the floor from a few feet away—the metal clink of a key dropping. Then the sound of it sliding against the floor.

"Thank goodness," my father said. "He found it."

I knelt and felt the floor near my feet and touched a small shoe. It was covering the foot of a child. I looked to see him standing there, right next to me with a key in his hand. It was a boy who had suddenly materialized out of nowhere.

"Here it is," the boy said, handing it to me.

I ran to the door, inserted the key, and the heavy doors unlocked. I took Forget-me-not from my father's arms, he took the hand of the boy, and the four of us hurried through.

Chapter 29—Souvenir

Carrying an unconscious Forget-me-not in my arms, I followed my father and the little boy without question. We were outside the building we had driven through and were following a rocky, narrow trail that led away from the building. It wasn't long before the building was out of sight. I struggled to keep my father and the little boy in my sight.

Though the air around us was cool, I fought to keep up despite my laboring breath. I could feel Forget-me-not shivering and wondered how I was going to keep her warm until we arrived at the maternity ward.

I caught up with my father and the boy, and thankfully they stopped for a moment so I could find out where we were going.

"Where is the maternity ward?" I asked, gasping. I leaned against the craggy side of the hill we were climbing. I looked around and could see no building in sight. I finally admitted my worst fear. "She's going to die if we don't get there soon," I said. I couldn't bring myself to add that the baby would die too.

My father gave a sensitive look to Forget-me-not. The little boy turned to me with a guileless look.

"Well Mr. Know-it-all," my father said. "You've gotten us into this mess. You don't know the way out?"

"Excuse me?" I said, sinking down, exhausted from carrying Forget-me-not up a hillside at an apparently high elevation. "Weren't you the one who was driving? And that boy giving all of the direction?"

I set Forget-me-not on the ground as carefully as I could, trying to find a comfortable place for her. I knew I could go farther without a rest and not before I knew exactly where my father and the boy were leading us. The insanity of the journey needed to end. As bad as the lower level of the hospital had been, it was worse to be outside far away from any medical help and with the untamed elements threatening to do us in.

"Well, well, well," my father said.

Forget-me-not opened her eyes and tried to speak.

"My dear," I said to her. "Please, you shouldn't speak. It will only make you weaker."

She shook her head and continued, coughing as she strove to find her voice. "You see him now?"

"Who?" I said.

"The boy." She struggled to breathe again. "You can see him too?"

"I don't know where he came from, but yes, yes, I can see him. He's standing right next to my father."

"Tell me what you see of him, please? I need to know exactly what you see." Forget-me-not's eyes were wide open, but I knew she was blind. I'm not sure why she wanted a detailed description of the little boy, but to keep her calm in her remaining hours I described what I saw.

The little boy couldn't have been more than five or six. He was bony, his head knobby enough that you could see his lumpy scalp through his pale blond crew cut. His face seemed too wide and his mouth seemed too small.

"Tell me more," she said.

I told her he seemed like a real cute kid.

"I thought he might turn out like that," she said, and the little boy's face lit up. It seemed like it didn't take much to make him happy.

I wondered how it was that a woman with amnesia would have such hopes for a boy she couldn't remember or maybe never knew? I didn't want to admit there was nothing I could do for her, not medically at least. It was clear that she was in the last moments of her life.

The boy stood next to my father and I could see his skinny rib cage moving up and down with each breath. The kid was scrawny. I did not want to point that out to Forget-me-not. I got the impression she might blame me for that.

"I remembered something," she said. And for what was to be the last time that day, I saw her smile. I remembered how radiant her smile could be.

"What is it?" I asked.

She had briefly fallen unconscious again, but then came to, the smile never leaving her face.

"What is it that you remembered?" I asked again.

"I have a toy. It belongs to him."

The little boy approached with a knowing look. "Mama," he said. "Where?" He peered into her face with an intent look.

She mumbled, and he moved so his ear on her lips. "Where?" he asked.

He put his little hand deep behind the chest of her overalls, down where her enormous belly had been straining in contractions only moments before, where the baby would be coming out. His face lit up when he found what she'd told him was there, With a yank, he freed it. Instead of a squalling baby, he'd pulled out a stuffed toy.

"My giraffe!" the little boy said. "You found it, Mama."

She smiled. "It wasn't really lost. I was taking care of it for you."

"We should go," my father said, holding his hand out to the little boy. "We're almost there. It's just around the corner."

I wasn't sure I could take another step.

Just then, Father came over and reached out to Forget-me-not, helping her to her feet.

"But the maternity ward…" I said. "Is that what's ahead?"

Forget-me-not stood up and adjusted the buckles on her overhauls. Her belly was once again flat. She took the boy's other hand and she and my father walked away, the little boy between them. I got to my feet with difficulty and followed them at some distance until they were out of sight. I stayed on the same path, grabbing branches and exposed tree roots to pull myself up a steep incline. When I came to the other end of the narrow path, it opened out onto a hilltop and no one was there.

I was all alone.

Chapter 30—Letting Go

Many years have passed since that tragic day Forget-me-not arrived in the emergency room with amnesia and we wound up taking a nightmarish journey through the subterranean wing of a now-closed hospital. I did everything I could to save her, first from the lecherous and inept doctoring of the captain and Lara, then from that very strange sequence of events that prevented me from giving Forget-me-not the kind of medical care she needed. After that day, I left the hospital but went on to successfully practice medicine, saving many lives over the years.

I'm told that I committed an error that day. Whether it truly *was* a medical error remains in some dispute. Because of it, I was required to practice medicine outside of the country until other circumstances forced me into retirement. After I retired, I came back to this place, to this particular hill, and every time I stand in front of the graveyard entrance, the events of that day go through my head.

I'm confused now. I know it. Retelling that story always brings confusion. Knowing what I know about the fragile human mind and its vast capabilities of invention, I know this story sounds far-fetched to the rational mind. And even though I don't quite believe it myself, I know that every word I have told you is true and faithful to my recollection.

The fact is, I don't come to this graveyard to remember. I come because I am legally required to tell you what the inscriptions read on tombstone 26-A, and that is the only reason I stand before it now.

Thus, while I continue to protest my sentence, I carry it out and accept that I must continue to do so as my appeals have been exhausted. Even the medical ethics board no longer accepts any new casework submitted by Albert Park, M.D.

I stand near a semi-circle of columnar junipers, pruned so they spiral in whirling heavenward corkscrews. Before me there is a small monument (numbered 26-A) engraved with the names of three persons, only one of whom remains alive. I am legally bound to tell you who lies buried here.

They are:

Mary, Sweet Wife and Dear Mother

Brian, Beloved Son

* * *

Forget-me-not's memory was never recovered, but she insisted, with her dying breath that day, that she was indeed named Mary, and the boy was her son, Brian. I arrived at the hilltop where she and my father had walked with the boy, and it was my father who saw me first when I bent over in grief that erupted unannounced from deep within me.

I thought everyone had gone and left me there alone, so I was surprised to look up and see my father standing over me.

"Where did you go?" I asked him, not quite believing that he'd returned.

"Albert," he said, putting his hand on my shoulder. "You can't go on like this. You shouldn't come here. You know you shouldn't."

"Where are they?" I asked. My eyes burned from countless hours of crying. Sometimes I thought I might go blind.

"They're gone," he said. "You know that."

He was about to say something else. I did not want to ask what it was. I was afraid to ask. I feared the answer.

"Albert, you know where they are, and you know why."

I wanted to say to him that I didn't know and ask why he was he being so cruel. But I knew that was wrong, even though I didn't believe it.

"No," I said to him. "*You* know where they are, and *you* know why they are there. Take me where they are."

"Albert, you know I can't. You need to face that and let go." He started to walk away.

"You're giving up, aren't you?" I said to him.

"No, I'm not. I just can't do this anymore, son. They're gone. They've been gone a long time. Nothing can change that fact. They died in the balloon accident on Brian's fifth birthday. You can't pretend it's something else."

"No! The boy said she died in childbirth." I remembered what Forget-me-not said the boy had told her when he was still a ghost, still hidden to me.

"Albert. You know that's not true."

I stopped him again. "I remembered…" I began. "A fire. A terrible fire. Wasn't it a fire that killed them?"

Or perhaps it had been someone else.

"No," my father said. "You know there was no fire."

Then he said something that he'd said many times before, a story I didn't want to believe was true. "You paid for the ride, but at the last moment, you decided not to go. They perished, son."

I remembered my father, the motorized cart, the long drive through the winding corridors. Had there been an accident on that ride?

"Your mind is playing tricks on you," he told me. "I drove the three of you to the hospital. Brian was next to me in the front seat, you and Mary in the back."

Yes. But I had dreamed all of that—my father driving us, Mary's fractured skull in my lap, bleeding and beautiful Mary. My little son Brian, already gone, crumpled in a broken heap in the front seat of the car. The quick but unnecessary drive to the hospital.

The memory, or nightmare, of that shattered day came back in flashes.

Before that day, nothing is clear. The man I am came to be after that day. That's all I know. That is all I want to remember.

"Albert, you need to let go of them. You make me bring you here every day, believing them to be here on this hilltop where the balloon was supposed to land. But they aren't here, Albert, and none of your fantasies about them being alive can change that."

My father holds out his hand, helps me get to my feet, and walks me back down the hill. On the way, we pass the long-closed hospital where I began my storied career as a world-famous neurosurgeon. I learned everything there is to know about the human mind, its capacity for creating great works of genius, inventions of madness. I always look to a particular set of windows that look out onto the surrounding town, the small park with an obelisk. It's there I swear I can still see her—a blind girl wearing oversized denim overhauls, heavy laced work boots with thick soles, and a hand-knit wool beret. She is wandering through the empty hallways guided only by ghosts.

Epilogue

Forget

"Wow," you say as you enter my darkened apartment. "The key still works, after all these years."

"I'm surprised you kept it," I say as I continue to watch a slide carousel turn on its spindle. Each slide flashes on the projection screen, and I let each one play for three seconds, before pressing the button to let the next slide drop in.

You walk up and sit next to me looking at the projection screen and I can smell your perfume.

Click, pull out the viewed slide, drop in the new one. The loud fan of the motor. The next slide comes up on the screen.

"You smell nice," I say.

"It's your favorite. Don't you remember? I always wear it. Lily of the valley."

You tell me how people associate the lily of the valley with a "return to happiness." You say you've told me that hundreds of times. You laugh. Or maybe you start to cry. I still want to touch your face, wipe away your tears, but I know you would find such a move irritating.

Why is it that the moment the truth is within your reach, you no longer want it?

I remember a conversation we had, perhaps it was last week, perhaps it was years ago. You've told me before that sentiment was unique to me.

Everyone else in the entire world, you've said, is capable of accepting the truth. But never Albert Park.

Everyone, I'd said. *You always exaggerate.* And you always laughed at my attempt at humoring you.

Click, the next slide advances.

"Oh. That's a nice one," you say. "All of us in the same slide."

I see you, me, two other boys.

"That was—let me think—graduation day." You laugh a little. "Graduation from kindergarten. I can't believe he was ever that tiny. Just look at all of us. I can't believe we were ever that young."

Click, the next slide advances. I can feel the warm air from the slide projector blowing on my hand. "See what I mean?" she says. Now I see you, me, two other young men. "Same group, another graduation day."

"Brian and Peter send their love," you say. "Isn't it strange that out of the four of us, those two stayed together all these years?"

You sit a while longer, watch all the slides, tell me the names of people in each slide. "That's me, Mary. That's you. There's Peter. There's Brian."

The four same people show up in every slide. They attend birthdays, parties, and go on vacations together. They show up in wedding finery.

"Oh, wait. Leave that last slide on a while longer. It's the park, isn't it, by the house?" She walks next to the screen and reads some of the words on a plaque in the photo.

There is a place called Albert Park. It lies in a triangle of land bordered by a strip mall, a dry cleaner, and a service garage. According to the plaque affixed to the monument there, (a 30-ft high obelisk modeled after the Washington Memorial) it is the world's smallest dedicated park. This designation is listed in Ripley's Believe It or Not. Look it up. Drive there and see it for yourself.

"That's right. Albert Park. You were fixated on it at one time." You look at me, blinded in the bright light of the projector in your eyes that are the strangest shade of faded gray. I see the tears in your eyes and say nothing.

The slide show is over. You open the shades, let the bright light into the room.

"Where'd this thing come from?" You point to the shelf in my room where a small stuffed giraffe sits. "And all this other stuff? I thought you sold all of it at a garage sale years ago."

I look where you are pointing and see the giraffe along with several other objects—a Zorro lunch box, a sand-filled balloon, a paint-by-number Jesus, a box of business cards for The Emporium of the Future You, a comic book and a pot of tiny flowers.

"Forget-me-nots," you say. "Are they real?"

You lift the little pot and sniff the tiny flowers, touching a few of the petals with your fingertips. "They seem so real, but I'm not sure." You examine them longer, holding them in the light coming through the window. "Can you tell me that story again about them? It's one of my favorites."

You sit in the chair next to the window, the one that looks out onto the town, and I tell you another story of my life.

Do you remember, Albert Park? A voice says.

I point out the grammatical error, take my red editing pen and strike through it.

The comma is unnecessary, the one between 'remember' and 'Albert.' Address the world, not me. Ask what it remembers of me. I remember everyone, everything. The faulty memory lies elsewhere.

Do you remember Albert Park?

About the Author

A native Minnesotan, Susan Koefod spent much of her girlhood taking long bicycle rides and walks through hilly Dakota County and along the Mississippi River. Such excursions typically filled her imagination with poetry and story ideas. She invariably thought of herself in the third person, fictionalized herself in her early stories, but relegated herself to the background as she could always invent more interesting characters to play the starring roles.

Susan Koefod is an award-winning novelist. Her Arvo Thorson mystery series debuted with *Washed Up* which was praised by Library Journal as "a smashing debut with astute observations and gorgeous prose." Her young adult debut is *Naming the Stars*. She has also widely published prose and poetry in numerous literary magazines, anthologies, and online venues. She is a winner of a Loft McKnight Artist Fellowship for Writers. She lives in West St. Paul, Minnesota, with her family.